KUROKO

"Tetsuro Shigematsu is one of the city's best artists, and *Kuroko* might be his most ambitious play yet."

    —ANDREA WARNER, *Georgia Straight*

"A new play from Vancouver's Tetsuro Shigematsu is always an event. Like his previous sold-out hits, *Empire of the Son* and *1 Hour Photo*, *Kuroko* is produced by Vancouver Asian Canadian Theatre and weaves together technology and deeply personal experience."

    —JERRY WASSERMAN, *Vancouver Sun*

"This is that rarity, a perfect play for a family – parents with their teen or adult offspring – to attend together ... *Kuroko* is a nuanced tale, well told by a skilled storyteller ... Don't miss it."

    —LORRAINE GRAVES, *Richmond Sentinel*

"Tetsuro shows himself to be a world-class lateral thinker, master of startling transitions. He can turn on a dime from intimate detail and wry self-mockery to cosmic musings on the karmic implications of the global water cycle or what earth's four-billion-year evolution might look like from the moon."

    —LINCOLN KAYE, *Vancouver Observer*

ALSO BY TETSURO SHIGEMATSU

EMPIRE OF THE SON
1 HOUR PHOTO

Both published by Talonbooks

KUROKO

A PLAY BY

TETSURO SHIGEMATSU

FOREWORD BY
JESSA ALSTON-O'CONNOR

INTRODUCTION BY
HEIDI TAYLOR

AFTERWORD BY
MARK ROBINS AND THE AUTHOR

TALONBOOKS

Talonbooks
9259 Shaughnessy Street, Vancouver, British Columbia, Canada v6p 6r4
talonbooks.com

Talonbooks is located on xʷməθkʷəy̓əm, Sḵwx̱wú7mesh, and səl̓ilwətaʔɬ Lands.

First printing: 2020

Typeset in Minion
Printed and bound in Canada on 100% post-consumer recycled paper

Cover artwork by Terry Aaron Wong
Interior cover sketches by Christine Reimer
Interior production photos by Raymond Shum
Interior design by Typesmith

Talonbooks acknowledges the financial support of the Canada Council for the Arts, the Government of Canada through the Canada Book Fund, and the Province of British Columbia through the British Columbia Arts Council and the Book Publishing Tax Credit.

Canadä   Canada Council   Conseil des arts   BRITISH   BRITISH COLUMBIA
              for the Arts   du Canada   COLUMBIA   ARTS COUNCIL
                                                                      An agency of the Province of British Columbia

Library and Archives Canada Cataloguing in Publication

Title: Kuroko : a play / Tetsuro Shigematsu ; foreword by Jessa Alston-O'Connor ; introduction by Heidi Taylor ; afterword by Mark Robins and the author.
Names: Shigematsu, Tetsuro, author. | Alston-O'Connor, Jessa Riel, writer of foreword. | Robins, Mark, writer of afterword.
Description: Text in English; includes some text in Japanese and Korean.
Identifiers: Canadiana 20200202804 | ISBN 9781772012699 (softcover)
Classification: LCC PS8637.H522 K87 2020 | DDC C812/.6—dc23

For my *kuroko* 黒子, Bahareh

CONTENTS

FOREWORD

BY JESSA ALSTON-O'CONNOR

How can a story feel unfamiliar one minute then deeply familiar the next? What is more real – the connections we make in the virtual world or those we forge face to face? Experiencing Tetsuro Shigematsu's *Kuroko*, I was confronted by these questions. The family of characters on stage took me to places entirely new, both physically and virtually. Yet as the play unfolded, I was drawn in by reminders of moments, feelings, or struggles I have encountered before but had never put into words. This is one of the strengths of Tetsuro's work – his ability to transport audiences to places where they feel seen or heard, often in unexpected ways.

I first met Tetsuro almost a decade ago, and since then I've seen his plays break box-office records across Canada, even selling out runs here in Vancouver before they actually open – a feat almost unheard of in Canadian theatre. We met through the literature and art communities – me coming from the art museum world, him from the literary and theatre scenes. Where my work lies in engaging audiences with ideas in visual art, Tetsuro's resides in storytelling and performance. Through different creative disciplines, our work deals in stories, in communicating ideas, and in harnessing art's ability to move us so that we may better understand ourselves and our times.

Tetsuro's plays defy expectations. For one, Asian Canadian theatre is never expected to break theatre records. His work stands out in a country where Asian voices and experiences remain too often non-existent in mainstream media and cultural discussions. Despite the fact that Asian communities have been part of Canadian history since the 1700s, today they still remain under-represented, or entirely invisible, in many areas of Canadian arts and culture. In Canadian theatre, Asian Canadian voices are seldom those writing or producing. The praise Tetsuro's work has garnered from critics and audiences alike demonstrates just how powerful and widely appreciated these under-represented stories and voices can be.

Whether one-man shows or shows with ensemble casts, Tetsuro's works have the astute ability to draw in audiences from across cultures. They offer journeys that oscillate between the familiar and the unfamiliar, blending the culturally specific with the universal. *Kuroko* is a story about a Japanese family whose members are worlds apart, separated by deep pain from their pasts and presents. We meet a father who feels his family is better off without him, and a daughter who is a *hikikomori* 引き籠もり – a severe recluse who retreats fully into the virtual world, shunning the physical reality around her. We follow a mother's struggle to cope with the loss of her missing son, a loss she can't move on from, and her fears for her daughter's social standing in life. Their family is torn apart, with little hope or trust in each other or in any future. But slowly they rediscover an instinctive desire to save one another. And in doing so, they change in ways few thought they would.

Tetsuro weaves this story with a balancing of humour, vulnerability, cultural layers, and a blend of storytelling techniques to bring experiences to life on stage that captivate and resonate with Asian audiences, especially Japanese Canadian ones. Members of these communities see their experiences and hear themselves on stage in a way that is rare in Canadian theatre. For some it may be their first time *ever* seeing or hearing their cultural experience reflected on a Canadian stage.

Tetsuro also defies outdated expectations that Asian Canadian theatre must be "niche," when in fact his work has demonstrated very clearly just how powerfully Asian Canadian stories can and do resonate beyond cultural lines. His stories are shaped by distinctly Japanese Canadian experiences and references, but in a way that shows diverse audiences how they, too, can see themselves in the struggles and experiences of a Japanese family. As I thought about writing this piece, I reached out to ask Tetsuro about this aspect of his practice: How does a playwright dance this fine line of cultural specificity, knowing the diverse audiences who attend his shows? How has he approached writing intentionally Asian Canadian stories that resonate across cultural lines and across Canada? "As for writing for Asian audiences," he told me,* "at times I would be writing specifically for Japanese Canadian audiences, and sometimes specifically for a subset who could understand Japanese. As someone who lived in Southern California and watched TV there, I liked tuning into programming like the BET cable channel and *not* understanding the cultural references. It was a reminder that the world was so much larger than the circles I was already privy to."

In *Kuroko*, Tetsuro expands the cultural groups he writes "for" by also bringing in characters shut away from the physical world who choose to be immersed in online gaming culture and virtual-reality communities. The culture of gaming and VR, as with any cultural reference, may feel familiar to some and completely alien to others. For many today, online experiences and even friendship or relationships are part of daily life; for others, venturing into gaming and VR feels utterly foreign. For most, stepping into the online world of a reclusive *hikikomori* feels even more unknown. Through *Kuroko*, Tetsuro brings audiences and characters into a story set in both a current-day Japanese city and a VR environment, where we follow characters

---

* All quotations by Tetsuro are reproduced from our personal email conversation in March 2020.

venturing into material and digital realms, each finding shared experiences in unexpected moments.

No matter the cultural context or setting, Tetsuro relishes how audiences of various cultural backgrounds respond:

> I think it made for a more interesting experience for the audience. Sometimes the balcony of high-school students [seeing *Kuroko*] would erupt with laughter at a particular reference, then a cluster of *Nikkei** sitting in the orchestra section would laugh, then the gamers would at something else. The radio jingle for *radio taisō†* would have been a mind-blowing moment for anyone who grew up with it. It was like the audience were eighty-eight keys on the piano, and the text would only hit certain cords at different moments. For me, it was sometimes just a matter of texture: the use of particular Japanese words or gamer jargon adds texture, and audiences can always infer the meanings without getting lost. But for those who are initiated, the pleasure they feel can be immense. The same way that internees hearing the names of their camps being called in [my previous play] *1 Hour Photo* enabled them to feel seen, because they had never heard those syllables spoken out loud on stage by an actor in the spotlight.

I'm not Japanese Canadian, nor do I game online, and so for me, watching *Kuroko* unfold, I felt a constant pull between recognizing and discovering references that were familiar one

---

*   *Nikkei* 日系 are the members of the Japanese diaspora – emigrants from Japan and their descendants that reside in a new country.

†   In Japan, *radio taisō* (or *rajio taiso*) ラジオ体操 are calisthenics radio broadcasts that play music with vocal guidance for listeners to follow along and exercise. They began in the 1920s and are still heard today.

minute and quickly lost on me the next. This oscillation – that pull toward the familiar and then back to the outside again – is intentional for Tetsuro:

> I think the key for me as a storyteller is to take audiences into worlds that are ostensibly unfamiliar: war-torn Japan, the Internment, virtual worlds … But populated within those worlds are, hopefully, characters and relationships that feel uncannily familiar. It is the sense of experiencing something novel, yet realizing it as an emotional landscape you recognize, like knowing where the streets lead in your dreams, because you've dreamt of this place before, even though it has no counterpart in real life.

Kuroko audiences discover and navigate a layering of textures, relationships, cultural references, and personal moments that resonate in different ways throughout the theatre, but that ultimately bring us to a place where we can explore deeper questions and experiences we all face. Through the journey he takes us on, Tetsuro's characters navigate with us complex challenges for which there are no simple answers. When we lose what gives our lives purpose, when the distance between ourselves and our families seems impossible to bridge, where do we turn? Can virtual worlds offer real solutions? Is death better than living a meaningless life?

In different ways, they and we each may feel alone in the "real" world and in the virtual ones, unsure of the way back home. How do we find our way back to ourselves, to each other, to our lives, when it feels like there is nothing left in this world for us? *Kuroko* layers a story across cultures, and across material and virtual realities, searching for something "real" in the places we least expect it, and it brings audiences along. It is a story that offers possibilities for building bridges when connection seems impossible, and it explores the powerful potential of healing others while saving ourselves.

INTRODUCTION

KUROKO: AVATARS IN (THE) SUICIDE FOREST

BY HEIDI TAYLOR

The creation of *Kuroko* was a journey into the unknown. As dramaturg on *Empire of the Son* and *1 Hour Photo*, I had the privilege of working in studio with Tetsuro Shigematsu as he developed stories on his feet. He directly addressed the audience and conjured worlds and situations from storytelling and visible sleight of hand. From hundreds of fragments, with the collaboration of director Richard Wolfe and the tremendous design teams, Tetsuro created jewel-box worlds to expertly tour his audiences through. For *Kuroko*, Tetsuro envisioned a full-length play that would feature a cast of at least five Asian actors. He would explore virtual reality and representations of suicide in Japanese culture, inspired by the 1721 play *The Love Suicides at Amijima* (*Shinjū Ten no Amijima* 心中天網島) by Chikamatsu Monzaemon 近松 門左衛門. Chikamatsu is considered the Shakespeare of Japanese literature, and the kabuki version of the play has inspired numerous retellings, including the Japanese new-wave filmmaker Masahiro Shinoda 篠田 正浩's 1969 stylized adaptation of the story as *Double Suicide* (*Shinjū: Ten no Amijima* 心中天網島).

Kuroko would develop characters and a narrative in a way that Tetsuro's previous projects didn't require. I was immediately intrigued. Vancouver Asian Canadian Theatre committed with Playwrights Theatre Centre (PTC) to an in-depth development process, and Tetsuro joined me as a PTC Associate writer-in-residence to dive into the project. The play's initial title was "Suicide Forest."

I visited Aokigahara 青木ヶ原 in February of 2018. I had not (and have not) watched much of the popular culture representations about the forest, also called the Sea of Trees (Jukai 樹海), that straddles the base of Mount Fuji 富士山 in Japan. Using GPS and my host's general knowledge of the area, we found a nondescript parking lot and walked icy pathways in bright sunshine. We looked at small shrines in the lava pockets that yawn darkly in the landscape and tried to integrate the socio-cultural significance of this ancient forest in popular and traditional Japanese culture with our relatively uneventful trip. With birds chirping, traffic audible, and the sun streaming through leafless trees in the still-winter landscape, the forest felt neither scary nor remote, though there are much deeper paths to explore. Researching representations of Aokigahara, popularly called Suicide Forest, brought me to a complex understanding of the shifting ideas of suicide in Japanese society, the commodification of Japanese culture on the global internet, and the intersection of economics and social status in how people around the world develop – and lose – their sense of self-worth.

Meanwhile, Tetsuro was developing characters and stories to interweave these thematically driven explorations into a play. The Chikamatsu inspiration quickly fell away in favour of more contemporary source material. One of his main characters, Maya, became a lens to explore the social phenomenon called *hikikomori* in Japan. Literally "pulling inward," this extreme reclusiveness, while most documented in Japan, has appeared around the world, especially as economic gaps widen and access to online life increases. As young people respond to increasing social and economic pressures by retreating to their rooms, cutting off contact with the outside world (except through online gaming), their middle-aged parents are confronted with the need to support adult children while sustaining themselves into retirement. These tensions began to clarify between a young woman who has lost her drive to live in the world, and her father, who discovers life is worth living only after deciding to die.

Through workshops with actors and director Amiel Gladstone, the thematic explorations developed into a family drama infused with Tetsuro's signature wit and irreverence. From a starting place examining what lurks in the symbolic dark forest of a society, Tetsuro began to investigate what lurks in the darkness of a family. While the initial source material for "Suicide Forest" was connected to the narratives of that supposedly eerily quiet place, deeper research into what drives suicide in Japan took us into different kinds of silence – community silence about economic failure, familial silence about grief, and individual silence about social exclusion. The humble tool that punctures these silences arrived from virtual reality – the chats and mediated dialogue of online gaming. We started on a new exploration: What is the difference between the unexpressed and the inexpressible?

Through VR tours and conversations with Alan Jernigan of Charm Games, Neil Kandalgaonkar of VR Chat, Athomas Goldberg of Pepper's Ghost, and cast member (and gamer) Lou Ticzon, I began to better understand the culture of virtual reality. This research revealed that the social interactions in game spaces were more germane to the plot than the mechanics of specific games. In the VR/gaming world we can construct avatars that reflect our identities. Folks living with barriers to communication or in isolated places can find like-minded friends in contexts that support communication. And in Japan, the growth of access to online communication has resulted in *hikikomori* receiving peer-led assistance to reintegrate back into society. The characters in the play began to argue the pros and cons of immersion in game space, and to play out a relationship of growing emotional intimacy online, complicating a simplified math where games equalled social isolation.

Developments in gaming technology continue to drive toward sensations of embodiment – the liveness that is core to theatrical experience. There are arguments for and against gaming as a meaningful social interaction, but what is clear is that gaming technology is powerful. The intent of the creator and the user will impact whether games bring us closer to our identities, imaginations, and communities, or whether they shroud us in dark spaces from which we are reluctant to emerge. Regardless of the social consequences of gaming, the creation of game spaces as places where bodies move in literal space – together but apart – reveals the craving for an experience that has not yet been recreated online. Presence is still sought after and approximated through increasingly sophisticated means, particularly with virtual reality headsets.

How can virtual reality be represented on stage? For this production, the constraints included costume changes on stage with no breaks, one set, and limits on video projection due to sightlines in the theatre. Through design workshops, director Amiel Gladstone and the design team arrived at a vision of the game space as a metaphor, allowing the emotional life of the characters to drive the kind of game spaces that would give the audience access to their transformations.

Another kind of silence emerged in the play that argues for shared embodied experience as a building block for emotional connection. John Ng, playing Hiroshi, watched Kanon Hewitt as Maya at the end of the *Dance Dance Revolution* scene (scene 13 (October), "*DDR*"). Maya dances with total unselfconsciousness in her virtual world, a smile on her face emerging from under her goggles for the first time. The audience witnesses the difference between the expert moves of the avatar, and the naive, enthusiastic dancing of a young woman who hasn't danced in at least five years. Hiroshi moves gently to the rhythm of the dance, nods, and turns away. His goal, to puncture his daughter's isolation and lead her back to the world, has worked. But the payoff for that success is that it brings him closer to ending his life. Nothing is simple.

The geographic Suicide Forest (Aokigahara/Jukai) merged in its representation in the play from a literal cultural site to a symbolic place of grief. It's the place that Hiroshi has inhabited since his son Ichiro's disappearance, the place that Kenzo visited in his own moment of despair, and the place where the Tanaka family must finally confront the unexpressed grief that has separated them from each other and compounded their suffering. The darkness that created veils between the characters takes on its own power, independent of the forest.

Who is the "kuroko" of the play? Tetsuro literally translates *kuroko* 黒衣 as "child of darkness," and the *kuroko* of Japanese theatre is, like a puppeteer onstage, responsible for transforming the space and assisting actors in accomplishing impossible physical acts in full view of the audience. The traditional *kuroko* costume is the source for the culturally appropriated "ninja" costume of countless films. In the play *Kuroko*, every character behaves as a *kuroko* in the drama of other characters' lives; their tasks, though, are primarily selfless actions taken on to improve the lives of others. Perhaps the ultimate invisible performer in Japanese contemporary culture is the actor hired out by a family rental agency to play a role in a real person's everyday life. From wedding guests to substitute parents, the professional performer may take on a one-time appearance or a recurring role. While hired mourners and other social functionaries are common cross-culturally, the contemporary rental-family-service (*rentaru kazoku* レンタル家族) phenomenon in Japan recasts the *kuroko* stage metaphor, as actors slip invisibly into the real life of an agency's client. "Better than real life" could be a slogan both for the virtual worlds inhabited by Maya and Kenzo and for the family units augmented by actors. Maya, as the child of grieving parents and as a *hikikomori* enshrouded in unhealthy isolation, links all of the characters, and through her transformation, frees her parents to act. Emerging from the literal darkness of her nocturnal existence as a gamer, Maya steps into adulthood and agency through the interventions of the *kurokos* in her life – Hiroshi and Kenzo.

At the moment of writing, our world has been transformed by a global pandemic, and social isolation has put us all into a test of how physical distancing impacts emotional intimacy. The social space of games has experienced a surge of participation, as people look for ways to connect while physical distancing keeps us physically safe. When theatres reopen in whatever form, I look forward to new productions of *Kuroko* that will be read in relation to all our desires to hide and to be seen, and to the unique place of the stage to explore and plumb these human needs.

During Japan's economic boom period, corporate *salarymen* サラリーマン were celebrated as the contemporary equivalent of mighty samurai warriors. Nowadays, many *salarymen* lead lives of quiet desperation (John Ng as Hiroshi).

Photo: Raymond Shum

(above) Masks in theatre are nothing new. Avatars online are common-place. But theatre masks representing online avatars? These are the small joys of collaboration.

(below) Imagine this photo in colour. Maya (Kanon Hewitt) drenched in a pale lavender light. Her parents Naomi and Hiroshi (Manami Hara and John Ng) bathed in the warm cast of 1970s Kodachrome film.

Photos: Raymond Shum

(above) One of the things I love most about theatre is how it can fold reality. It can show two disparate actions unfolding simultaneously in the same space. (From left to right: Manami Hara, Kanon Hewitt, and Lou Ticzon.)

(below) Just as most Americans believe in angels, the Japanese believe we are surrounded by spirits. It is simply a given. (Kanon Hewitt and John Ng.)

Photos: Raymond Shum

PRODUCTION HISTORY

Kuroko was first produced by Vancouver Asian Canadian Theatre and developed at Playwrights Theatre Centre as part of the PTC Associates program. It was presented in the Historic Theatre at The Cultch in Vancouver, British Columbia, from November 6 to 17, 2019, with the following cast and crew:

MAYA TANAKA: Kanon Hewitt
HIROSHI TANAKA: John Ng
NAOMI TANAKA: Manami Hara
KENZO KANEDA: Lou Ticzon
MS. ASADA: Donna Soares

Playwright: Tetsuro Shigematsu
Director: Amiel Gladstone
Producing Artistic Director: Donna Yamamoto
Dramaturg: Heidi Taylor
Set Designer: Sophie Tang
Lighting Designer: Gerald King
Costume Designer: Christine Reimer
Projection Designer: Remy Siu
Assistant Projection Designer: Daniel O'Shea
Sound Designer: Sammie Hatch
Production Manager and Technical Director: Adrian Muir
Stage Manager: Susan Miyagishima
Apprentice Stage Manager: Kitiya Phouthonesy
Props Master: Jennifer Stewart
Cultural Consultants: Mayumi Yoshida, Manami Hara, and
    Taizo Shigematsu

CHARACTERS

MAYA TANAKA
a woman in her early twenties

HIROSHI TANAKA
a middle-aged *salaryman* サラリーマン

NAOMI TANAKA
a middle-aged homemaker

KENZO KANEDA
early twenties, a *Zainichi* 在日, Korean living in Japan

MS. ASADA
mid-thirties, the CEO of a rental-family agency

SETTING AND TIME

Tokyo 東京
Now

All photographs were taken by Raymond Shum at
The Cultch's Historic Theatre in Vancouver, BC
(November 6 to 17, 2019).

KUROKO

(above) What do you become in a world where you can be anything? Maya and Kenzo (Kanon Hewitt and Lou Ticzon) frolic in the freedom of anonymity.

(below) Why does Hiroshi (John Ng, with Donna Soares) look this way? Because, as they say, you are only as happy as your unhappiest child.

Photos: Raymond Shum

Family Romance

HIROSHI stands alone.

An electronic bell chimes, and HIROSHI goes in through an entrance.

MS. ASADA
Welcome.

> *Together they bow and exchange their business cards using both hands.*

> *MS. ASADA's business card is golden.*

HIROSHI
Ms. Asada. "Better than real life." That's quite a promise.

MS. ASADA
Mr. Tanaka. What can we do for you?

HIROSHI
My situation is ... How do I put this?

MS. ASADA
Mr. Tanaka, let me assure you I've been in this line of work for a long time. There's nothing you can tell me that would shock me. I know it's not easy being a man in Japan these days.

HIROSHI
I'm not here for me. It's my daughter.

MS. ASADA
Does your daughter have a name?

HIROSHI
Maya.

MS. ASADA
Oh! That's my sister's name. And how old is Maya?

HIROSHI
Twenty-three.

MS. ASADA
And is Maya an only child?

HIROSHI
She has an older brother.

MS. ASADA
Just two kids?

HIROSHI
Yes. We had our children very far apart.

MS. ASADA
I see. And who do you think Maya could use in her life
right now? A girlfriend to go shopping with? A boyfriend
to see the cherry blossoms? Grandparents? A new mom?

HIROSHI
No.

*MS. ASADA begins swiping through some
profiles on a tablet.*

MS. ASADA
How about an older sister? I have just the actress. She
recently joined our company, but I think she'll soon be in
high demand. Better to book her now while you still can.

HIROSHI
Maya isn't well.

MS. ASADA
Oh?

HIROSHI
She's at home. She's *always* at home. She is *hikikomori*
引き籠もり. She won't leave her room.

MS. ASADA
No, yes. I'm, I'm quite familiar with the phenomenon. I
watched a documentary on NHK.

HIROSHI
Right. That. Don't worry, she's not dangerous.

MS. ASADA
It said there are over three million *hikikomori* in Japan?

HIROSHI
I only know one.

MS. ASADA
I see.

5

HIROSHI
So can you provide someone to befriend our daughter?

MS. ASADA
How does Maya spend her days?

HIROSHI
Sleeps. At night, she plays videogames.

MS. ASADA
And how long has she been in her room?

HIROSHI
Well, she hasn't been to school in ... My goodness, it's been five years.

MS. ASADA
Why now?

HIROSHI doesn't follow.

MS. ASADA
I'm not saying things must be great at home, but I imagine they're pretty stable. Why the sudden need?

HIROSHI
She's twenty-three. I need her out on her own within a year.

MS. ASADA
This is for her? Or you?

HIROSHI
Let's focus on my daughter.

MS. ASADA

Mr. Tanaka, I find the more honest a potential client is willing to be with me, the better I'm able to help them.

HIROSHI

Yes, of course.

MS. ASADA

Do you have ... cancer?

HIROSHI

No. Worse. I lost my job.

MS. ASADA

I'm so sorry.

HIROSHI

One year from now, I'm planning to ... make an exit.

MS. ASADA

For the insurance payout?

HIROSHI

I realize it's not the most original plan.

MS. ASADA

Let's just say you're not the first laid-off *salaryman* サラリーマン to come up with such a scheme. You are aware, the fine print usually stipulates that no benefits will be paid out if the insured commits suicide within two years of taking out a policy?

HIROSHI

Not my coverage. I only have to hold off until the end of
the year. Before I go, I need to know my daughter will be
okay. That way I can have peace in my next life.

MS. ASADA

Does your wife know about your plans?

HIROSHI

The less she knows the better. Can you provide a friend for
my daughter?

MS. ASADA

Mr. Tanaka. When we used to deal with families like yours
in the past, we found that the underlying problem wasn't
with the *hikikomori* themselves, but with those *around*
them. Parents pay us to fix their child, not to ask *them*
about their own childhoods.

HIROSHI

I just don't know what else to do. There's no medication
she can take, no electroshock, no lobotomy. There's
nothing physically wrong with her that'll show up on an
MRI. Some say this is a symptom of the culture at large, a
national malaise, whatever that means. All I know is, we
used to be a normal family.

MS. ASADA

I wish there was something I could do for you.

HIROSHI

(*standing up*) Ms. Asada, you run a rental family agency.
(*thrusting back her business card*) My daughter just needs
a friend.

MS. ASADA

As I said, we no longer take on *hikikomori*.

HIROSHI

If it were your daughter, what would you do?

MS. ASADA

(*hesitating at first*) The Dingo Manga Café デイ ンゴ マン
ガ喫茶. It's full of *otaku* オタク. Ask for Kilroy37.

> *MS. ASADA writes this down on her business
> card and hands it back to HIROSHI who stuffs
> it in his pocket.*

HIROSHI

Every time I think I'm approaching the finish line, it gets
moved back.

MS. ASADA

Mr. Tanaka, may I say – and take this as you will – in my
experience, it's okay to be scared. It means something
incredible is about to happen.

The paradox of disguises is that they grant us the freedom to reveal who we are. Kenzo and Maya play a form of truth or dare.

Photo: Raymond Shum

Dancing as Fast as I Can

KENZO wears the most expensive "skin" and protective battle armour money can buy. He is armed with a gleaming assault rifle. A mask obscures his face. his face. He is an online avatar.

From a crouched position, he slowly rises. Gun fire and explosions. Out of desperation, KENZO starts dancing.

MAYA, also in avatar form, rises.

MAYA
Are you a bot, or just a system glitch?

KENZO
These moves do wonders for me in *Dance Dance Revolution* ダンスダンスレボリューション.
I'm hoping they might save me here.

MAYA
You hoped wrong.

MAYA raises her weapon.

KENZO
Don't kill me!

MAYA

Did you just say "Don't kill me"?

KENZO

I'm not even supposed to be here! I don't even like first-person shooters.

MAYA

Then let me show you the exit.

KENZO

Can you please not kill me? I have a question that only you can answer, and if you kill me you'll never learn what it is.

MAYA pauses.

KENZO

Why do I never see it coming?

MAYA

This is a hot zone. More combatants, more combat.

KENZO

Will you teach me?

MAYA

Why would I do that?

KENZO

Enlightened self-interest? It's this crazy idea that people who serve the interests of others ultimately serve their own self-interest. It's the understanding that what you do to enhance the quality of *my* life will ultimately enhance your own.

MAYA
Sounds like bullshit. I play alone. Always have.

       MAYA chambers a round.

KENZO
I'll pay you.

MAYA
How?

KENZO
Bitcoin?

MAYA
You have cryptocurrency?

KENZO
No.

       MAYA turns off her safety. KENZO drops to his
       knees, with his hands raised in surrender.

KENZO
Goddamn VR is no different than RL. Underdogs like me never get any mercy from Alphas like you.

MAYA
Did you just call me an Alpha?

KENZO
You don't know what it's like to be bullied your whole life. I was born to lose.

KENZO starts to cry.

MAYA

Stop crying. Watch streamers. KillSwitch and Ninja99. Learn from their play style. See that guy in the distance?

KENZO

The one who ducked behind the dumpster?

MAYA

When he pokes his head out, he's going to come out on his right.

KENZO

How do you know?

MAYA

Because he's right-handed. If he leans out from the left, he'll have to expose his entire body to get a shot off.

They watch the player run off.

KENZO

Why didn't you take the shot?

MAYA

Never shoot unless you're sure you can make the kill, otherwise you draw attention to yourself. Some enemy squad will make our location, and RPG us when we reload.

Always arrange your weapons the same way in your inventory. When you go through a door, close it behind you. Don't move through open spaces. Stay low, zigzag.

KENZO

What if I found a hiding spot, and just stayed perfectly still?

MAYA

No one likes a Bush Wookie. Camping might prevent you from dying, but it's no way to live.

KENZO

Are you for real? You're just so cool. I feel like I'm talking with an anime character.

MAYA

(*unaccustomed to compliments*) Okay, I think my work here is done. Um ... Good luck.

MAYA runs.

KENZO

Looks like you're headed in the same direction I was gonna go. What a coincidence!

KENZO runs.

WELCOME HOME

It is nighttime at the Tanakas', a Western-style home in Chiba 千葉, a suburb of Tokyo. HIROSHI walks up to the house wearing his overcoat.

HIROSHI
Tadaima! ただいま！

(*to himself*) How are you? How was your day?

I'm fine. How was yours?

It's good to see you father. Thank you for all your hard work.

Don't mention it. It's a father's duty to take care of his family, *especially* his daughter.

(*outloud again*) *Tadaima!*

NAOMI
(*entering*) *Okaerinasai!* おかえりなさい！

When HIROSHI isn't looking, NAOMI discreetly smells his coat before hanging it up.

NAOMI
How was work?

HIROSHI
Same.

NAOMI

Tell me about your day.

HIROSHI

Always the same. (*awkwardly*) How was *your* day ... today, *okāsan* お母さん?

NAOMI

How nice of you to ask. Come, sit down for dinner.

HIROSHI

I'm not hungry.

NAOMI

I made your favourite. *Okonomiyaki* お好み焼き.

HIROSHI

So tired.

NAOMI

From what?

HIROSHI

I told you. Work.

NAOMI

Hiroshi. Stop lying.

> *HIROSHI stays silent.*

NAOMI

How did you think you could possibly hide this from me? I do all the finances. Why have your paycheques stopped being deposited?

HIROSHI
I didn't know how to tell you.

NAOMI
You lost your job?

HIROSHI
"Managed out."

NAOMI
Did they give you any kind of severance?

HIROSHI
Six months.

NAOMI
That buys us a little time.

HIROSHI
That was three months ago.

NAOMI
You've been getting dressed for work every morning!
Where have you been going?

HIROSHI
I walk. When it rains, I duck into the Kinokuniya 紀伊國
屋 in Shinjuku 新宿区 to read books about our daughter's
condition.

NAOMI
While I'm stuck here actually taking care of our daughter?

HIROSHI
Any change today?

NAOMI
What do you think?

HIROSHI produces a book.

HIROSHI
This one has been my favourite so far, full of practical
advice. I was too embarrassed to hand it over to the
cashier. So I went ahead and ... borrowed it.

NAOMI
It's not enough you're unemployed, now you're a thief? I
should have listened to my parents.

NAOMI takes the book from him.

HIROSHI
I think you might find it interesting.

NAOMI
You need to return this.

HIROSHI
There's actually a group of us at the bookstore. We don't
know each other's names, but we nod hello. When
someone stops showing up, no one says anything, but
we're all thinking the same thing. Maybe they found a job,
but more likely they made a decision.

NAOMI

You have *one* responsibility, to take care of your family. What are we going to do? We barely have any savings.

HIROSHI

We have the house.

> *NAOMI stares at HIROSHI carefully as he goes to their bedroom.*

> *NAOMI is alone. HIROSHI has left his suit jacket. NAOMI begins to put it away, when she discovers MS. ASADA's golden business card.*

ABANDONED BUILDING

MAYA and KENZO are in the room of an abandoned building. KENZO tags the walls with "Kilroy37," while MAYA is crouched by a window, scoping out the view.

KENZO shakes his spray can. She does not look at him.

MAYA

(*annoyed*) What are you doing?

KENZO

Tagging up turf. You want me to make one up for you? Or do you already have a tag, "CobraKali"?

MAYA

Better to leave no trace.

KENZO

Why?

MAYA

Listen. I helped you. Now I'm done.

KENZO

We're just two people having a conversation.

MAYA

Did you hear something?

21

KENZO
Hear what?

MAYA
Footsteps. Shut up.

KENZO
My mom hears things. Smells things, too. She's always complaining that her car smells like McDonald's.

MAYA
I really don't care.

KENZO
When she goes shopping in Ginza 銀座, her driver has no time to grab anything else. So I told her, if you want Akio to eat something other than Big Macs, give him a raise.

MAYA
Wait. Your mom has a limo driver?

KENZO
He's not a limo driver. He's just this guy who works for my dad. And it's not a limousine. It's more of a town car.

MAYA
Limousines are stupid. The only people that drive around in them are yakuza やくざ, the Emperor, and people like my grandpa. You want my advice? No one respects pay-to-win posers like yourself.

KENZO
If weren't for us, you free-to-play types wouldn't have anyone to look down on.

MAYA

You pay big bucks for the shiniest weapons, and you don't
even know how to use 'em.

KENZO

I may not be a pro at first-person shooters, but I bet I
could teach you a thing or two about networks.

MAYA

I play alone.

KENZO

When we ran over here, I noticed some latency in your
avatar. I'll bet you're not on Ethernet are you? Wi-Fi is fine.
Just make sure you got a clear line of sight between you
and your router's antenna. Better signal. Better gameplay.
You're welcome.

A grenade gets tossed into the room.

MAYA

You left the door open, didn't you?

The sound of an explosion.

UP and aT 'Em

HIROSHI is fully dressed for work, rushing to get out of the house. He takes a sip of coffee and grabs his briefcase. NAOMI watches him as she neatens a stack of papers.

NAOMI
Going somewhere?

HIROSHI stops. He's been playing this charade so long, he has to think about this.

HIROSHI
Well, I guess I have something of a routine by now.

NAOMI
Right, you mentioned your little book club, but it isn't raining today. Where were you planning on going?

HIROSHI
I was planning on making a visit to the library. I've been reading about simulation theory. It's this idea that you and I might not actually be real.

NAOMI
I don't need a book to tell me that.

HIROSHI
I'm going to check if there are any new publications on *hikikomori*, latest treatments. Then maybe have my bento

down by the river. I'm thinking about heading to the unemployment centre.

NAOMI
(*laughing at the futility of it*) Now that you don't have to put on a show for me anymore with your suit and tie and your empty briefcase, I can finally leave the house. I've written a list of chores. Don't put them off, because there will be a different list for you tomorrow.

NAOMI hands the list to him.

HIROSHI
(*reading*) Clean out the gutters, power wash the driveway.

NAOMI
Don't think of them like chores. Think of it as a home-based workout.

NAOMI puts her papers in her purse.

HIROSHI
What's that?

NAOMI
My résumés.

HIROSHI
What should I do for lunch?

NAOMI
That's the fridge. Find something you like. Put it in your mouth.

HIROSHI
    And Maya?

NAOMI
    Whatever you make her, leave it on a tray outside her door.
    Then hide. She will only grab it if she doesn't see you.

HIROSHI
    Don't worry. I'll heat up some miso on the stove.

    *NAOMI gathers her things and heads for the
    door.*

NAOMI
    The fire extinguisher is under the kitchen sink.

    *NAOMI steps out of the house, ready to take on
    the world.*

NAOMI
    Ittekimasu! いってきます！

    HIROSHI is left to himself.

    *MAYA slowly peers out her door to see what's
    changed in the house. She and HIROSHI make
    eye contact, and she quickly looks away and
    retreats into her room.*

    HIROSHI doesn't know what to do.

SCENE 6 (MAY)

FIREMAN'S CARRY

KENZO forms a human bridge on his hands and feet. He is stuck.

MAYA quickly enters, not looking at him.

There is a flash of lightning, followed by thunder. MAYA spies something coming at them.

MAYA
Incoming!

MAYA dives to the ground. Sound of an explosion, followed by a burst of automatic gunfire.

KENZO
Help! I don't know how to let go of this thing!

MAYA ducks under KENZO and mounts her weapon on his back.

KENZO
What are you doing?

MAYA
Using you as a shield.

KENZO
I don't know how I feel about that!

There is a flash of lightning, followed by thunder.
MAYA spies something coming at them.

MAYA
Incoming!

MAYA and KENZO dive to the ground.
Sound of an explosion, followed by a burst of
automatic gunfire. They both try to get up, but
KENZO still can't. MAYA is also having trouble.

MAYA
Ah! My feet must have caught some shrapnel.

KENZO
Now you know how I feel!

MAYA
I need you to get us out of here!

KENZO
How?

MAYA
Stand up and carry me. Oh man. Stand up, then hit X to
engage and lift.

KENZO
(*standing up*) X.

KENZO reaches for MAYA and pulls her onto
his shoulders, fireman's-carry style.

MAYA
Now run!

KENZO spins in a circle.

MAYA
Pick a direction and run!

KENZO stops spinning and begins running. Like a rear gunner, MAYA shoots those behind her.

MAYA
I got 'em!

KENZO stops and turns around.

MAYA
Don't stop! Keep running!

THINGS ARE DIFFERENT NOW

NAOMI returns home, while HIROSHI turns on the dishwasher.

NAOMI looks at HIROSHI expectantly.
HIROSHI returns her gaze with a blank stare.

NAOMI
(*exhausted*) *Tadaima!* After three weeks of handing out my résumé, every business owner in Chiba knows your wife is looking for work. I'm going to have to find some ways to cut household expenses. Money saved is money earned. Isn't that what they say? I might even sell one of my kimonos.

HIROSHI
Hurry! We need to hide.

NAOMI
In here?

NAOMI and HIROSHI move to a disused bedroom.

HIROSHI
Shhhh. She's about to come out of her room.

NAOMI
But it's day time.

HIROSHI
Things are different now. She's picking up on it.

NAOMI
What's different?

HIROSHI
You. You haven't been home at this time for the past few ·
days. She doesn't know your rhythms.

NAOMI
My rhythms?

HIROSHI
After Maya finishes her breakfast at two, I get her tray and
I watch *Kurashiru* クラシル to get some ideas of what
to make her for her five-o'clock lunch. Then I run the
dishwasher. That's her cue that the rest of the house will be
empty for at least an hour. That's her time to come out.

NAOMI
Usually she skulks around only at night.

HIROSHI
It's a recent development. She flips through newspapers,
magazines. The last few days she's made it to the kitchen
counter.·

NAOMI
We have to wait in this room for an hour? I feel like a
prisoner in my own house.

HIROSHI

Now you know how she feels. I think my next step is to
encourage her to come out and talk to me.

NAOMI

How are you going to do that?

HIROSHI

I don't know yet. (*looking around*) Did you remove some
of the things in here?

NAOMI

I gave a few things away. I read that preserving a son's
bedroom can prevent closure.

HIROSHI

We're not preserving his room. We're *keeping* it for him.

NAOMI

Yes, of course.

> *HIROSHI picks up an RX-78-2 Gundam ガンダ
> ム toy robot. NAOMI takes it from him and puts
> it away.*

HIROSHI

Where did you put all his trophies?

NAOMI

(*lying*) I'm not sure.

HIROSHI

MVP? Quarter-finals, National Junior High School
Baseball Championship?

NAOMI
I know the ones you're talking about. I was also there.

HIROSHI
Those weren't yours to give away.

NAOMI
(*slowly*) Hiroshi-san. Ichiro is not coming back.

Silence.

NAOMI begins to exit the space.

HIROSHI
Don't! She'll see you.

NAOMI steps out of the room. MAYA walks in.

NAOMI
Maya. How are you?

MAYA grabs a towel, covers her head, and sits down, hiding herself in it, rocking back and forth. HIROSHI pulls NAOMI into Ichiro's room.

HIROSHI
What are you doing? Do not talk to her. Don't even make eye contact. How is she ever supposed to trust us if we keep violating her boundaries!

NAOMI nods contritely.

NINTENDO POWER

MAYA is alone in game space. With no one to talk to she looks slightly bored. She discovers a "Kilroy37" tag on the wall.

MAYA
Here too?

KENZO spawns.

KENZO
Who are you talking to?

MAYA
Myself.

KENZO
At least when I'm around you appear less crazy.

A ruby-red laser dot appears over KENZO's heart.

MAYA
Sniper!

KENZO looks down at the ruby dot.

An impressive physical stunt from KENZO, which results in him returning fire with both hands.

The gaming environment responds with a fireworks display of over-the-top pageantry befitting victorious Roman generals. MAYA is perplexed.

MAYA
Wait. What happened?

KENZO
What?

MAYA
How did you do that?

KENZO
Practice.

MAYA
No.

KENZO
That's why you haven't seen me around. I've been working on getting worthy enough to be your partner.

MAYA
Partner?

KENZO
Sidekick.

MAYA
I've been playing this game since beta. That sniper was, like, pro level. But he couldn't get a bead on you.

KENZO

    Fast learner?

MAYA

    Oh *puleeze.*

KENZO

    Catlike reflexes?

      KENZO executes a dance move.

KENZO

    (*finger gunning*) Cheat code.

MAYA

    There are no cheat codes for this game.

KENZO

    There are according to *Dr. Saito's Strategy Guide.*

MAYA

    Wait, is that like one of those *Nintendo Power* magazines from back in the day?

KENZO

    I dunno, those were before my time. It's kinda like Konami Code 2.0, activates God Mode. Go into the root of the game folder, go inside "ASSC", find a CSV file called "prst", go to line 145, and make that zero a one. Locks your health bar to one hundred percent, and gives you maximum shields. Makes you invincible to all damage, with the exception of gunshots to the head. If someone has your skull in their crosshairs, it's still gonna get popped.

MAYA
Say the code again.

KENZO looks at her for a beat.

KENZO
Just buy it for yourself.

MAYA
Are you kidding me? After all the times I died because of you?

KENZO
I'm telling you, this guide is redonkulus! It shows how you can convert all your common weapons into uncommon, bolt-action into semi-auto, semi-auto into a fully automatic, single barrel into a double barrel, minigun into a light machine gun.

MAYA
Where did you get it?

KENZO
Akihabara 秋葉原.

MAYA
Where?

KENZO
Ask around!

MAYA exits the game.

MAYA writes something down on a piece of paper, and knocks on the wall.

*This attracts HIROSHI's attention. When she sees
he is approaching, she slips him the paper.*

*HIROSHI reads the note, puts on his shoes and
prepares to leave the house, just as NAOMI
comes home, carrying the* hikikomori *book and
some groceries.*

NAOMI
Going somewhere?

HIROSHI
Our daughter is sending me out on an errand.

NAOMI
An errand? She actually *spoke* to you?

HIROSHI shows the handwritten note.

NAOMI
(*reading*) "Go to Akihabara. Buy *Dr. Saito's Strategy Guide*.
Ask around." Strategy for what?

HIROSHI
I don't know. I'm going to ask around.

NAOMI
Is it me, or has Maya become a lot more chatty online?

HIROSHI
She said things before.

NAOMI
She made angry noises occasionally. I figured she was losing.

HIROSHI

Maybe now she's winning.

NAOMI

Yes, but winning what? A boyfriend?

HIROSHI

Would that be so bad?

NAOMI

(*ignoring this, as she puts down her grocery bags*) If I do all my shopping after 7 p.m., just before closing, the supermarket marks down ready-to-eat foods as much as fifty percent!

HIROSHI

Fifty percent?!

NAOMI

If only my mother could see me now. I don't think in her whole life she ever stepped foot inside an OK Supermarket.

HIROSHI

Of course not. All of her shopping would have been done by servants.

NAOMI

Help. We had *help*. You're not working. I'm not working. We can't eat my *obi* おび. Which reminds me ... (*showing him her smartphone*) What are all these e-transfer payments?

HIROSHI

I'm not sure.

NAOMI

    Regular withdrawals from our account. I better call the
    bank.

HIROSHI

    Those are me. I'm the one making those withdrawals.

NAOMI

    Do you mind telling me what they're for? (*silence*) Who *is*
    she?

HIROSHI

    Pachinko パチンコ. All those colourful lights, the music
    blaring, all those little steel balls rolling around. I used to
    look down on all the losers who spend all day there, but I
    have to tell you, *pachinko* is strangely addicting.

NAOMI

    But you hardly leave the house.

HIROSHI

    Online. I've been playing *pachinko* online. I know it's
    pathetic, but I'm going to get a handle on it.

NAOMI

    You're not playing *pachinko* online. (*showing Ms. Asada's
    golden card*) Who is Ms. Asada? "Better than real life"! I
    know what that means!

    NAOMI tosses the card on the table.

HIROSHI

    No. You don't.

NAOMI
(*waving Maya's note*) Stay here. I'm going to Akihabara to
find this Dr. Saito. Maybe *he* can tell me what's really going
on. And while I'm out, the only young women you should
be spending time with is your daughter.

> *NAOMI puts the book in his hands and leaves
> the house.*

> *HIROSHI reads from the book.*

HIROSHI
"Once minimal communication has been established, avoid
asking open-ended questions. Inquiries that require one-
word answers are best."

> *MAYA removes her gaming headphones.*

HIROSHI
I don't know what to cook for dinner, Maya. Do you feel
like *tonkatsu* 豚カツ or tempura 天麩羅 tonight?

> *Pause. HIROSHI slowly goes to the kitchen.*

MAYA
Curry.

> *HIROSHI stops. He nods slowly, before rushing
> to the kitchen.*

> *MAYA emerges from her room. She picks up Ms.
> Asada's business card that NAOMI has left on
> the table and retreats back into her room.*

(above) "As if you could kill time without injuring eternity" —Henry David Thoreau. Maya and Kenzo prepare to take out a high-ranking combatant.

(below) Just as a tycoon can step over the homeless lying on the sidewalk, you can live in the same house and yet inhabit different worlds.

Photos: Raymond Shum

BaTTLe RoYaLe

*MAYA and KENZO occupy a sniper's nest.
KENZO peers through a pair of binoculars.
MAYA stares through the scope of a long-range
sniper rifle.*

MAYA
Range.

KENZO
Five hundred metres.

MAYA adjusts the top dial on her rifle's scope.

MAYA
Wind.

KENZO
Seven to eight. East to west.

MAYA adjusts the side dial on her rifle's scope.

KENZO
Between the right and left windows.

MAYA
Got him. Come to Daddy.

KENZO
You realize who you got in the crosshairs, don't you?

MAYA
I can read.

KENZO
He's always top of the leaderboard. If we kill DevilDog, we're gonna crack the top ten. We'll be famous!

Meanwhile, HIROSHI begins turning on house lights one by one. The house is getting brighter and brighter. Using a handful of remotes, HIROSHI turns on the AC, the TV, the stereo, and then a hair dryer. Poof! A fuse is blown.

Their home and the VR game are plunged into semi-darkness. KENZO disappears altogether. Only MAYA and HIROSHI are half visible.

MAYA
(*panicking*) No!

HIROSHI
We must have blown a fuse.

MAYA
I'm gonna die!

HIROSHI
Sorry?

MAYA
Two people are going to die!

HIROSHI
What do you want me to do?

MAYA
You're the dad!

HIROSHI
Right. Reset the breaker!

MAYA
Yeah! Do that!

HIROSHI
I don't know where it is. Do you?

MAYA vocalizes in frustration.

HIROSHI
Come out and help me find it.

MAYA vocalizes in frustration even louder.

HIROSHI
You know, Maya, I'm actually okay with the darkness. We can save money on utilities.

MAYA runs out of her room, drags her dad to a far wall, indicates the breaker panel, and runs back to her room. HIROSHI opens the panel and throws a switch.

MAYA respawns to sniper position with KENZO. He drops his binoculars momentarily.

KENZO
Where did you go?!

MAYA

What's happening?

KENZO

The next time you disappear like that, leave behind your sniper rifle. I can't do much damage with my sidearm. Not at this range.

MAYA

Where's our target?

KENZO

(*resuming surveillance*) First floor. The last muzzle flash came from the left window.

MAYA

Windage?

KENZO

Same. Seven to eight, east to west.

MAYA double-checks her top scope.

KENZO

He's aiming at us!

A distant shot rings out. MAYA fires her weapon. There is a large recoil.

MAYA

Pink mist.

KENZO

That's it? Are we the only two left?

MAYA

(*slowly*) And then there was one.

MAYA chambers a round in her pistol.

KENZO

Hey, hey. Let's talk this through!

She shoots KENZO in the head.

As the echo of the gunshot subsides, it is replaced by the electronic thrum of music, signifying victory.

A shift in light. MAYA and KENZO are no longer in the battlefield, but in "The Lobby." They smile at each other.

KENZO

No need to apologize. No hard feelings. I'm just happy together, you and I got to –

MAYA

I've never won a battle royale before.

KENZO

Yeah. You're welcome. So how do you feel?

MAYA

Honestly? Kind of empty. Kind of stupid.

KENZO

So in other words ...

MAYA
Same as before.

KENZO
Funny, me too. I mean, how long did that take? For us to get good enough to notch our first victory?

MAYA
Playing as a duo? I dunno. Took a while.

KENZO
How many first-person shooters have you mastered?

MAYA
Doom, *Wolfenstein*, *Call of Duty*, *Duke Nukem*, *Halo*, *Quake*, *BioShock* ...

KENZO
My point is, you've played a lot of FPS games, right?

MAYA
Yeah, so?

KENZO
You've got some leet skills. But did you ever think, what would happen if you were dropped into a real-life combat situation?

MAYA
I'd die.

KENZO
How fast?

MAYA

Urban combat zone? Ten minutes. Nine minutes longer
than you, Dance Dance Revolution.

KENZO

I'm not just a dancer. I used to be obsessed with *Guitar
Hero.*

MAYA

Guitar Hero and *Dance Dance Revolution.* Got it.

KENZO

Anyway, I got to the point where I could do "Bohemian
Rhapsody," FC, 100 percent on expert difficulty. I could
even hit extended quads.

MAYA

I don't know what that means, but I assume you're
bragging.

KENZO

But the fact is, if someone handed me a baby ukulele, I
couldn't play "Twinkle, Twinkle, Little Star" if my life
depended on it.

MAYA

Right, so in other words you bat a thousand with a
controller, but if someone actually threw you a ball, it
would hit you in the face. Is that what you're trying to
stay?

KENZO

Nothing we master *here* helps us out *there.*

MAYA

(*shrugging*) I've never felt at home in the real world.

KENZO

Did you ever think ... maybe we're playing the wrong kind of game? I mean we spend all this time as avatars, wielding assault weapons, exploring different worlds, but maybe the most important thing isn't completed missions or frame rate or clock speed, maybe it's us.

MAYA

Okay ...

KENZO

To me the most interesting thing in the game ... is you.

MAYA doesn't know how to respond.

KENZO

We won our first battle royale today. How come?

MAYA

We worked as a team?

KENZO

I want to show you something. A place where you can feel alone but not lonely. It's a place I made for you. Meet me there.

KENZO walks away.

MAYA watches KENZO as he walks upstage.
When she turns around to face downstage,
MAYA is now wearing VR-style goggles, which

*she removes in view of the audience. She slowly
steps out into the living area.*

*MAYA sees HIROSHI. He has set a table for
two. HIROSHI sees her. He quickly improvises a
makeshift third setting for MAYA, who appears
to be considering this invitation.*

*NAOMI arrives home. She sees MAYA and
HIROSHI looking at each other.*

*NAOMI walks over and proudly hands MAYA
the gamer magazine,* Dr. Saito's Strategy Guide.
*The spell is broken. MAYA grabs it and retreats
to her room.*

SCENE 10 (SEPTEMBER)

WORMHOLE

MAYA and KENZO are in a blue-green abstract space. It feels like the canopy of a forest, but it isn't. It's like an underwater forest.

MAYA
What is this place?

KENZO
Exactly.

MAYA
What do you call it?

KENZO
It has no name.

MAYA
In other words, you don't know.

KENZO
Better to leave no trace.

MAYA
Whatever.

KENZO
Have you ever heard of a magic circle?

MAYA

Is this where I'm supposed to say, "No, but won't you please tell me"?

KENZO

A magic circle is a sphere beyond the usual rules of right and wrong. That sphere is here. I made this place so we could play wormhole.

MAYA

Wormhole? You mean like *Portal*?

KENZO

No, a new type of game. You know what a wormhole is?

MAYA

Yeah, a tunnel, or a shortcut thingy through space?

KENZO

Exactly. But not just space, through time *itself*. Theoretically, time travel *is* possible, but the amount of energy it would require to reach into the quantum foam and open even the tiniest portal for a nanosecond would exceed the energy that all the power stations on earth could generate.

MAYA

Keep talking like that and you're gonna stay a virgin.

KENZO

This wormhole game operates along these same principles. It recognizes the possibility that two people can take a shortcut through time and get to know each other better in an instant than most married couples who spend a whole

lifetime together. I know that must sound impossible
to you.

MAYA

Um, no. Have you met my mom and dad?

KENZO

So you wanna try?

MAYA

Well, if we're gonna quit murdering people, I guess we
better find something to kill time.

KENZO

I'm going to subject you to a lie detector test, but first I
need to collect some information about you. Name three
things you love ...

MAYA

Takoyaki 蛸焼き.

Beat Takeshi ビートたけし.

Overclocking.

KENZO

Okay, now you're just trying to flirt with me because you
know about my obsession for water cooling. Stand on one
leg like this. Dancing Shiva. Okay, without losing your
balance say, "*Zatōichi* 座頭市 is a great movie."

MAYA

Zatōichi is a masterpiece.

KENZO
Agreed. Now name three things you hate.

MAYA
Nattō 納豆.

Nosey neighbours.

People who aren't who they say they are.

KENZO is unnerved by this answer.

KENZO
Now say, now say, "I love *nattō*! Gooey, sticky, stinky *nattō*."

MAYA
I love *nattō*.

KENZO
Poopy, pissy, vomity *nattō*!

MAYA
(*laughing*) I love *nattō*!

MAYA falls over.

KENZO
See? Loss of balance.

MAYA
That's because you made me laugh.

KENZO
Or because you were *lying*.

MAYA

I get it. Fibs make you fumble. It's like your health bar
takes a hit. Your turn.

KENZO

What do I love? Water cooling, *Astro Boy* 鉄腕アトム,
forest bathing.

MAYA

Forest bathing? Typical. And what do you hate?

KENZO

Discrimination, bullies, daikon 大根.

MAYA

So you despise social injustice and fibre. Got it.

KENZO

Okay. Now we're going to do a little something I like to call
"Double Dancing Shiva." We're going to touch palms. And
together we're going to open up a wormhole that will allow
us to jump through time and get to know each other faster
than what should be humanly possible.

MAYA

And if one of us lies?

KENZO

Then we'll lose balance and the wormhole will collapse.
The portal will open the moment we achieve perfect
balance, just enough of an aperture to permit a single truth
to pass between us.

MAYA
A single truth? Who's to say if it's true?

KENZO
That's easy, because the truth is never what you expect.
And it wounds. This game is built on trust. Better to lose
your balance than your integrity. Now ask me anything!

MAYA
Have you ever fantasized about me?

KENZO
Yes. (*beat*) Have you ever fantasized about me?

MAYA
Yes.

The wormhole opens.

Radio Taisō

MAYA watches HIROSHI finish doing radio
taisō ラジオ体操, *traditional Japanese
calisthenics. Curious, MAYA stares at
HIROSHI's tattoo and touches her own arm.*

HIROSHI self-consciously covers it up.

HIROSHI
Oh yeah. Mummy hates it. Reminds her that I'm low caste.
The koi is a Buddhist symbol.

MAYA
For courage.

HIROSHI
Do you believe in reincarnation?

MAYA shakes her head.

HIROSHI
Me neither. But I heard a priest once say, or I dunno,
maybe it was one of my stupid managers, someone said,
when we die, and get reborn, we travel in small groups.

MAYA
Like families?

HIROSHI

Kind of. But we play different roles. Your grandmother
might become your nephew.

Or your daughter might become your only friend.

*MAYA reaches out and touches HIROSHI's
tattoo – the koi representing courage.*

*MAYA steps outside into the pouring rain.
NAOMI appears.*

NAOMI

Maya stop!

MAYA stops.

NAOMI

You need your coat.

MAYA

I wanna feel the rain.

*HIROSHI stops NAOMI. Together, they watch
her step outside into the rain.*

MAYA tries to look up into the rain drops.

*NAOMI stands with HIROSHI watching their
daughter.*

TOKYO SKYTREE

MAYA and KENZO are in a virtual outdoor amphitheatre, watching the end of a Beat Takeshi (Takeshi Kitano 北野 武) movie. Credits roll.

KENZO's fully upgraded armour and weapons are now gone, and have been replaced by low-level gear. MAYA is elated.

MAYA
Beat Takeshi's best ending ever.

KENZO
Pretty good.

MAYA
Pretty good? You know something better?

KENZO
No, no, you're right. I can't argue.

MAYA
Is someone else playing your avatar? What'd you do with Kilroy?

KENZO
It's me, it's me. Water cooling, *Astro Boy*, *shinrin-yoku* 森林浴.

MAYA
So what happened to your gear?

KENZO
What about it?

MAYA
You used to be fully strapped. But now it looks like you got mugged.

KENZO
A great warrior doesn't require the best weapons.

MAYA
Said no one ever.

KENZO
Where do you wanna go? I'll take you anywhere.

MAYA
In the world?

KENZO
Mmm ... Greater Tokyo Metropolitan Area.

MAYA
I always wanted to see the view from the top of Tokyo Skytree 東京スカイツリー.

KENZO
(*incredulous*) Shut up.

A ritual.

MAYA	KENZO
Takoyaki.	Water cooling.
Beat Takeshi.	*Astro Boy.*
Overclocking.	*Shinrin-yoku.*
Nattō.	Discrimination.
Nosey neighbours.	Bullies.
People who aren't who they say they are.	Daikon.

KENZO and MAYA are in an observation deck.

MAYA
Wait. Is this place what I *think* it is?

KENZO
This takes up way too much space on my drive, but I could never bring myself to delete it.

MAYA
Wow. You can see so far from here.

KENZO
It's even better at night.

It becomes night. They are gently underlit by the glittering lights of Tokyo.

KENZO
Back when Tokyo Skytree first opened, I spent an entire week just to be first in line for the grand opening.

MAYA

You camped outside for a week?

KENZO

I was what you call "between homes."

MAYA

Hard to believe you're still single.

KENZO

Said Ms. "I always play alone."

MAYA

(*contritely*) So you were the first person on the observation deck of the tallest building in the world?

KENZO

Tallest *tower*. Almost.

MAYA

What happened?

KENZO

It was a job. Some *oyaji* おやじ in a pinstripe suit wanted to impress his girlfriend – who was *my* age.

MAYA

Gross.

KENZO

By getting her in on opening day. So he paid me to line up.

MAYA

An entire week?

KENZO

Actually, the base of Tokyo Skytree is a great place to camp.
Get this: morning of, he comes up to me, looks up at the
tower ...

MAYA

He doesn't want the tickets.

KENZO

Yeah. How did you know?

MAYA shrugs.

KENZO

So I look up, too. It's so rainy, so foggy, you can't even
see the top. No wonder he didn't want to go up. He goes,
"Look around, there's plenty of pretty girls who would love
to be escorted to the clouds." And sure enough, there's
some high-school students my age, cuttin' class, smoking,
looking bored.

MAYA

I was one of them.

KENZO

Huh?

MAYA

I was one of them. I was there, too. Opening day. Cutting
class.

KENZO

What?! Are you *kidding* me? Are you messing with me?

MAYA

I was always cutting class. That day? It was the only place
to be.

KENZO

I can't believe it! I should have asked you. Would you have
said·yes?

MAYA

If you offered me a free ticket? For *free*?

KENZO

Of course!

MAYA

I dunno. Maybe. It'd be a coin toss.

KENZO

Those are good odds! I can't believe this. All my life, I
wondered what would have happened if I had asked one of
those sullen high-school girls, and you were one of them!
That could have been like our first date.

MAYA

Yeah, and just think, if you did, today you and I might be
married, with one and a half kids, and you'd be miserable,
and I'd be depressed, and we'd blame each other for our
unhappiness. You'd watch TV, and I would ignore you by
reading trashy romance novels, resenting every breath
you took, and wanting to murder you every single night
because of your snoring.

KENZO

Oh my god. That sounds amazing! You know how every little girl moons about meeting their one true love at the top of the Eiffel Tower in Paris?

MAYA

Not every.

KENZO

What do you moon about?

MAYA

I don't.

KENZO

Oh *come* on. You never dream about meeting that special someone?

MAYA

No. Never. I don't think it's in the cards for me.

KENZO

But if it was, who would it be?

MAYA

Do they have to be human?

KENZO

They can be anything.

MAYA

Chun-Li 春麗?

KENZO

Oh. Yeah, I always picked her in *Street Fighter* ストリートファイター. She's such a badass. Wait a sec, which version? Skinny Legs or Ms. Thickness?

MAYA

Thunder thighs all the way. The thought of Chun-Li's pythons wrapped around me. One clench? Pop my head off like a cork. I'd die happy.

Listening outside MAYA's room, NAOMI doesn't like what she has just heard. HIROSHI catches NAOMI eavesdropping.

NAOMI

Who's Chun-Li?

HIROSHI

Who cares? She's talking. That's a good sign.

NAOMI

But who is she talking to?

HIROSHI

Let's just be thankful that we can hear her voice.

MAYA enters the room and sits at the table at an empty place setting.

NAOMI and HIROSHI hold their breath.

HIROSHI and NAOMI quickly share their food into a third dish and slide it over.

MAYA starts to eat. The family eats together.

SCENE 13 (OCTOBER)

DDR

KENZO and MAYA are doing a two-person
Dance Dance Revolution (DDR) *routine using*
only their feet. There is a big EDM (electronic
dance music) finish, accompanied by intense
illumination. MAYA thrusts her finger up
toward a giant invisible scoreboard.

MAYA

See that? Perfect score. In your face. *DDR!*

KENZO

No, no, no. That was *not* dancing. That was you just
moving your thumbs.

MAYA

(*flicking her hand rhythmically*) In sync to the beat!

KENZO

Look, when I hacked this game so we could dance without
mats, it wasn't so you could play lying down. Yo, check it
out, my heart rate peaked at nearly two hundred beats per
minute. Yours never went above ninety. Were you taking a
nap?

MAYA

That's because I'm calm, cool, and collected, even when
I'm beating you at your own game.

KENZO

Did it ever occur to you that the point of this *dance* game might not be scoring points but maybe, I dunno ... *dancing*?

MAYA

Then why is it a *game*?

KENZO

To motivate you into actually moving?

MAYA

Fine, I'm still gonna beat you.

KENZO

Yeah, we'll see. Yo, DJ, drop that beat!

EDM music starts.

KENZO

Okay, here we go.

KENZO and MAYA start to dance the same dance, but this time using their whole bodies.

KENZO

See that? Your heart rate is actually climbing.

MAYA

That's because you're making me mad.

KENZO

Mad with lust.

MAYA

In your dreams.

KENZO

Where do you think you are? In! My! Dreams!

MAYA

More like a nightmare. Dammit!

KENZO

Don't worry about the score! You're not a pilot inside a
mecha メ カ. Just feel the beat!

*KENZO and MAYA dance. HIROSHI enters
and notices MAYA.*

WHO WAS ICHIRO?

*MAYA wanders into Ichiro's room. HIROSHI
watches her. MAYA senses she's being watched
and turns to see HIROSHI.*

MAYA is about to leave.

HIROSHI
Your brother has the best laugh. He laughs like an old man.

MAYA stops.

MAYA
I have memories, but I don't know if they're real.

HIROSHI
He was fifteen. You were ... four? His last year of junior
high. Popular, but for some reason he stopped spending
time with his friends. Just kind of withdrew. And then we
were all surprised when Ichiro suggested that we all go to
Fuji-Q 富士急 together. He wouldn't go on any of the rides
with me, just stood there and watched, with this smile.
Then when it was time to go home, at the last minute he
disappeared.

MAYA
Disappeared?

HIROSHI
He didn't say anything to me.

71

MAYA
What did you do?

HIROSHI
Police were useless. So I spent a lot of time studying maps, had them all spread out. I wouldn't let Mommy set the table for months. Finally the police told us it was possible he may have walked two and half hours ... to Jukai 樹海.

MAYA
Suicide Forest.

HIROSHI
Don't call it that.

MAYA
But that's what everyone calls it, Dad. It's the most haunted place in all of Japan.

HIROSHI
Your brother is not a ghost haunting Suicide Forest. You have to be dead to be a ghost. He's a missing person.

HIROSHI takes out his wallet and shows her a tattered photograph.

HIROSHI
He's my anchor.

MAYA looks at the photo for several moments as if trying to remember something. She hands back the photo to him. HIROSHI gestures that she should keep it.

Wordlessly, MAYA expresses surprise, then gratitude. She holds the photo of her brother against her chest.

HIROSHI
You would like him. And he would feel the same.

MAYA has made a decision. She stares intently at the photograph.

MAYA
If I walk down the driveway, will you come with me?

Together, HIROSHI and MAYA exit the house and walk down the driveway.

FOREST RANGER

MAYA and KENZO are in the blue-green abstract space.

A ritual.

MAYA	KENZO
Takoyaki.	Water cooling.
Beat Takeshi.	*Astro Boy.*
Overclocking.	*Shinrin-yoku.*
Nattō.	Discrimination.
Nosey neighbours.	Bullies.
People who aren't who they say they are.	Daikon.

MAYA and KENZO are on the roof of the Toranomon Hills tower 虎ノ門ヒルズ.

MAYA
Where are we?

KENZO
Toranomon. Tallest building in Tokyo.

MAYA
Right. Skytree is the tallest tower.

KENZO.

Yeah. But this time we're on the roof. No civilians are allowed up here. If you jumped it would take seven seconds to land on the ground.

MAYA

I'm not sure "landing," is the right term for it. Do you know anything about Jukai?

KENZO

Suicide Forest? What about it? It's not as scary as they say. That's for sure. Most of what you hear isn't actually true. You know how they always say it's the quietest place on earth because there are no animals in the forest? Not true. It *is* weirdly quiet, but I saw birds.

MAYA

You went there?

KENZO nods.

MAYA

How did you get there?

KENZO

Subway. Couple of trains. Then a bus.

MAYA

No limo?

KENZO

Nah, I slummed it with the people. Have you ever heard how if you take ten steps off the trail, turn around ...

MAYA

And you'll be lost forever? And GPS and compasses don't
work because the soil has too much magnetic iron in it
from Mount Fuji's eruption?

KENZO

Yeah, yeah, all that "Bermuda Triangle of forests" stuff
is BS. But, I will admit, I do *not* have the best sense
of direction, so just as a precaution, I went to Can Do
キャンドゥ, bought their biggest roll of ribbon, one
hundred metres. So there I am, past the "No Trespassing"
signs, past the warning signs ...

MAYA

"Life is a precious gift from your parents. Think calmly
once more about them, your siblings, your kids. Don't
keep it to yourself, please confide in someone."

KENZO

That's kind of weird that you'd have that memorized, but
whatever. So, I walk a few kilometres in on the main
trail. I figure, this is far enough, I must be in the heart,
so I tie one end of the ribbon to a tree, double knot, real
tight, and I begin making my way into the forest. Not easy.
The ground is, like, *super* contorted. I don't see how the
"undecided" can camp there overnight. You'd definitely need
a hammock. So, I'm walking along on this rotting tree, I
jump down, and what do I see in the hollow beneath? In
the dark, shadowy hole? I see an old ... sleeping ... BAG!

MAYA

(*laughing*) You're so stupid. I can't believe you got lost in
Suicide Forest.

KENZO

Spoiler alert. I *do* make it out alive. So, I begin making my way back, following the ribbon. Here's the thing ... I come to the *other* end of the ribbon, and it runs out. I'm holding onto the end, but it's no longer tied to the tree the way I left it. It's not tied to *anything*. It's been cut. No knot, no wrinkles, just cut.

MAYA

Was it the *yūrei* 幽霊?

KENZO

I don't know. I didn't see any spirits. So, there I am, standing in the middle of the forest. No trail. I don't know if Jukai is the most haunted forest in all of Japan, but it definitely has the most trash. Weird how people's last meal ends up being junk food.

MAYA

I suppose you run out of time, you run out of money, you run out of choices. Pocky ポッキー and C.C. Lemon (C.C.レモン) is better than nothing. It would suck to die hungry.

KENZO

Or alone.

MAYA

How did you get out?

KENZO

Maybe I didn't. Maybe I'm still there.

MAYA
Shut up. My dad thinks my brother is there.

KENZO
You have a brother?

MAYA
Yeah. Ichiro. I didn't know him, but I dream about him sometimes. He's eleven years older. He was.

> *Beat.*

KENZO
You want me to take you there? I could.

MAYA
No way.

KENZO
Maybe we should meet face to face first?

MAYA
Maybe.

> *MAYA reaches for her goggles and disappears.*

SCENE 16 (OCTOBER)

SAMUI さむい

NAOMI is wearing a light outdoor jacket, doing calculations at the table. HIROSHI enters the common area, looking cold, rubbing his hands.

HIROSHI
Is there a door open? Why is it so cold in here?

NAOMI
Because it's fall. It's supposed to be cold. Put on a coat. The good news is, I managed to find a buyer for our car.

HIROSHI
The bad news?

NAOMI
It's only enough to get us through December.

HIROSHI begins to put on his jacket and shoes.

MAYA enters.

HIROSHI and MAYA leave.

(above) Few things affect a daughter's psychological development more than "father absence." Hiroshi tries to make up for lost time.

(belòw) The legendary crowdedness of Tokyo subways is nothing compared to Japan's social pressures.

Photos: Raymond Shum

SCENE 17 (OCTOBER)

IRON TRIANGLE

MAYA and HIROSHI are walking. They stop outside a train station. Other commuters brush past them.

HIROSHI
We're going to take the train.

MAYA looks surprised.

HIROSHI
We're going to ride the Tōzai Line 東西線. And I'm not gonna lie. You may remember it as crowded, but now, it's even worse.

MAYA doesn't want to.

HIROSHI
Trust me. Tokyoites are so self-absorbed, you could have a seizure, you could be foaming at the mouth, and no one will notice.

MAYA looks skeptical.

HIROSHI
Believe me, what other people may or may not do will be the *least* of your concerns. You might suffocate! At this time, peak rush hour, it'll be well above two-hundred-percent capacity. Ribs break, people pass out. But they don't fall down! Remember what I taught you back in grade school?

MAYA
"The Iron Triangle"?

Uncertain, MAYA holds her wrist.

HIROSHI
That's good, but remember the key is to lock your elbows to the side of your rib cage. The Iron Triangle protects your breathing space. The Iron Triangle is your friend.

Are you ready?

MAYA shakes her head.

HIROSHI
It's okay to be scared. It means something incredible is about to happen.

HIROSHI grabs MAYA's hand, and they thread their way through the turnstiles, down the escalators, and into a crowded subway car.

EMPTY HOUSE

NAOMI comes home to an empty house. It is too quiet. She approaches MAYA's space.

NAOMI
  Maya?

> *NAOMI slowly enters MAYA's space and is surprised to find it empty.*

> *She looks around, and takes advantage of this rare opportunity to snoop around in MAYA's private lair. She spies MAYA's VR goggles. She gingerly tries them on.*

> *She finds herself in an abstract world of KENZO's creation.*

> *MAYA trips as she spawns into being. The actor playing MAYA embodies this scene, but we hear the voice of the actor playing NAOMI. KENZO is excited to see her, but tries to act nonchalant.*

> *NAOMI-AS-MAYA marches around in circles robotically.*

KENZO
  What's wrong with you? Are you having a stroke?

NAOMI-AS-MAYA
  Hmm?

(above) Think reading someone's diary is bad? At one of *Kuroko*'s performances, a collective howl rose from a cluster of students as they watched Naomi step into Maya's avatar.

(below) Maya and Kenzo stand on the tallest building in Tokyo, but it's really VR, but it's really a play, but it's really a photo.

Photos: Raymond Shum

KENZO
You look like you're sitting on your controller.

NAOMI-AS-MAYA runs into a wall, again and again.

NAOMI-AS-MAYA
(*whispering*) Just a second.

Finally, NAOMI-AS-MAYA stands very still, facing away from KENZO.

KENZO
Why are you whispering?

NAOMI-AS-MAYA
My parents are nearby and listening.

KENZO
And you forgot how to type "P.A.L."?

NAOMI-AS-MAYA
How long have we known each other?

KENZO
Apparently not long enough.

KENZO tries to start the ritual.

KENZO
Shall we assume the position?

KENZO poses in Dancing Shiva.

NAOMI-AS-MAYA
What position do you want me in?

KENZO
Wormhole?

NAOMI-AS-MAYA
Is that where you stick your worm, in my...

KENZO
What?! What is wrong with you?

NAOMI-AS-MAYA
How do I delete you?

KENZO
Your voice sounds really ... Wait. What did you say?

NAOMI-AS-MAYA
I don't think we should talk any more.

KENZO
What's going on? Who *are* you?

NAOMI-AS-MAYA
(*cutting him off*) Let's meet in real life.

KENZO
IRL?

NAOMI-AS-MAYA
No, in real life.

KENZO
Yeah, that's what I said.

NAOMI-AS-MAYA
Do you want to get together or not? Face to face.

KENZO
Where do you want to meet?

NAOMI-AS-MAYA
Somewhere in public?

KENZO
How about ... Yachiyodai Park 八千代台近隣公園?

NAOMI-AS-MAYA
That's ... in my neighbourhood.

KENZO
I know. Three hundred metres south-west.

NAOMI-AS-MAYA
How do you know where we live? Have you been here
before?

KENZO
(*shrugging*) Voice chat is client-to-client, and I just
Wiresharked your IP address. Don't be creeped out that I
creeped on you. Paranoid much? Okay ... What time?

NAOMI-AS-MAYA
Now.

KENZO
    ASAP?

NAOMI-AS-MAYA
    No, as soon as possible.

        HIROSHI enters the house, relishing his bubble
        tea. He's never been so happy.

HIROSHI
    Tadaima!

        NAOMI scrambles to remove the goggles. She
        exits MAYA's space quickly.

NAOMI
    Where's Maya? She's not with you?!

HIROSHI
    (*exuberant*) We took different routes home.

NAOMI
    Are you *trying* to lose her?

HIROSHI
    She wanted to go to see the Gundam robot statue. It was
    quite peaceful, watching it light up like that.

NAOMI
    So nice you could have a moment of calm, while I'm here
    at home having heart palpitations.

HIROSHI
Sorry.

NAOMI
No you're not.

HIROSHI
You know, spending so much time with Maya ... Have you
told your parents about our situation?

NAOMI
You know what my dad said to me when he realized I was
going to go through with our wedding? He said, "I no
longer have a daughter." But I didn't care, because I had
you, and then when we had Ichiro, I had my *own* family.
So what if our home life made Korean soap operas seem
dull, it was my family. I *had* a family.

HIROSHI
You still have a family. And Maya is getting better.

MAYA comes back, but her parents don't see her.

NAOMI
And now you want me to go grovelling back to the one
person I despise most on this earth, show him what a mess
my life has become, and beg him for money?

HIROSHI
No.

NAOMI
If I didn't have you and Maya to take care of... I need to
go out.

HIROSHI
Now?

NAOMI
Yes.

> NAOMI exits and MAYA emerges. What did
> she hear?

> MAYA goes into her room.

PLAYGROUND

*KENZO sits perched on the playground backlit
by the sodium-vapour lamps of the street lights.
He looks cold. NAOMI enters wearing a hoodie
that hides her face.*

KENZO
Part of me wanted to bust out some *DDR* moves for you
when you came around the corner, but I didn't know how
long you'd be.

> *NAOMI removes her hood. KENZO is taken
> aback. He stands up.*

NAOMI
You're a lot younger than I thought you'd be.

KENZO
Whoa. And you're a lot older.

NAOMI
I'm Maya's mother.

> *KENZO is stunned. He bows deeply.*

KENZO
Maya?

NAOMI
You know she's not well, don't you?

91

(above) Just like the rest of us, Maya sees phantoms everywhere, projected onto the world by the magic lantern of her imagination.

(below) It's never easy meeting the parents, but when you're a Korean meeting an old-school Japanese mother? Good luck with that.

Photos: Raymond Shum

KENZO

What do you mean?

NAOMI

She's *hikikomori*.

KENZO

I've known that the whole time.

NAOMI

It's all well and good that you two have hit it off online,
but I'm trying to get Maya *out* of the house. I can't have
someone like you be one more reason for her to never
leave her room.

KENZO

Someone like me?

NAOMI

Guys like you.

KENZO

You mean *Zainichi* 在日?

NAOMI

Wait. You're ... You're Korean?

KENZO

People always eventually find out. Whatever.

NAOMI

I'll have you know I'm not like other Japanese. I happen to
think that your people are, are ... very good-looking. Your
K-pop idols, Jisoo 김지수, Chaeyoung 손채영 ...

KENZO

Yeah, that's great. Thanks.

NAOMI

Look, it doesn't matter who you are. You could be the
Crown Prince of the imperial family. Maya's just not ready
to be in a relationship.

KENZO

You don't even know your daughter. How much time have
you spent with her?

NAOMI

Her whole life.

KENZO

All you see is Maya blindfolded by goggles, but I've seen
her lead armies.

NAOMI

Your world isn't real!

KENZO

Why? Because it's made up of ones and zeros and not
atoms and molecules? Maybe the world is changing too
fast for your liking, but the truth is, the change has already
happened. We're building a new world, based on *who* we
are, what we *do*.

NAOMI

Maya is my daughter. I am her mother. If you really care
about Maya, you will leave her alone.

SCENE 20 (DECEMBER 31)

FORBIDDEN FRUIT

MAYA and NAOMI are both holding plastic shopping baskets filled with food items to celebrate the New Year: prewrapped sashimi platter, cuts of fish in styrofoam and saran wrap, and other traditional New Year's foods. They move forward slowly in line.

MAYA

Why don't people just do their grocery shopping on December 30? Why does everyone wait till December 31?

MAYA flips through a K-pop magazine.

NAOMI

They're just like us. They don't plan ahead. I know you've met a boy online.

MAYA shoots her a look.

NAOMI

You don't know anything about him. He could be *Korean*. Have you ever considered that?

MAYA

He's *not* Korean.

NAOMI

Well, how do you know that? Have you ever asked him?

MAYA

I wouldn't care.

NAOMI

You don't care that someone would deliberately misrepresent themself to you?

MAYA

The whole point of being online is so we don't have to meet. And what if we did meet? What if he's totally hot? Plus his family is, like, filthy rich. Just like yours. Doesn't that make you happy?

> *HIROSHI joins them in line carrying two tall cans of Japanese beer.*

NAOMI

Why would you think that would make me happy?

MAYA

So I don't make the same mistake you made marrying Dad, which you did just to get back at your parents, and now you regret it because now you're cut off from them and now you don't even have any friends because you're too ashamed of your daughter, who is nothing but a freak who will never get better.

HIROSHI

Maya. Everyone can hear you.

MAYA

What? You're not exactly helping. You lost your job and you'll never work again. What are you good for?

NAOMI

Maya. Let's talk about this at home.

MAYA

I know you wish we would both just die already so you
could finally be free.

NAOMI

Stop.

MAYA

I know you and Dad didn't want me. And you wonder why
Ichiro went to Suicide Forest?

> *MAYA throws down her shopping basket and
> runs out of the grocery store.*

NAOMI

Maya, please!

> *NAOMI and HIROSHI are left alone to pick up
> after her and endure judgmental stares.*

RUSH HOUR

MAYA is running. She isn't sure where to go.

She pulls out Ms. Asada's golden card.

MAYA follows other commuters to the station entrance.

MAYA holds the Iron Triangle as she is lifted up by fellow commuters.

New Year's Eve

*MS. ASADA is alone in her workplace,
concentrating on counting out a stack of crisp
ten-thousand-yen notes, before inserting them
into colourful* otoshidama おとしだま *New
Year's envelopes.*

MAYA stands alone. She fiddles with her phone.

An electronic bell chimes, and MAYA goes in.

MS. ASADA
Welcome. Can I help you?

MAYA shows her the business card.

MS. ASADA
Someone gave you my card. (*giving Maya the once-over*)
Did you bring a headshot and résumé?

MAYA gives her a disapproving look.

MS. ASADA
Oh. I'm sorry. What can I do for you?

MAYA
(*reading the card*) "Better than real life"? What does
this mean?

MS. ASADA

That's our company slogan. I am Ms. Asada.

MAYA

Why did my father have your card?

MS. ASADA

I meet a lot of fathers. And mothers. What's your dad's name?

MAYA

Tanaka, Hiroshi.

MS. ASADA

Oh! You must be ... Maya. I'm so sorry.

MAYA

(*interrupting*) Why did my father have your card?!

MS. ASADA

We exchanged cards when we met.

MAYA

Why would my dad come to see you?

MS. ASADA

Your father was concerned about you. He didn't know where to turn. I just pointed him toward someone who could help him.

MAYA

(*suddenly realizing*) Kilroy37?

MS. ASADA
    You know him?

MAYA
    You told my father to hire Kilroy37?

MS. ASADA
    No, I told your father to go to the Dingo Manga Café.

MAYA
    (*vocalizing her frustration*) I don't know what's real
    anymore!

    MAYA heads for the exit.

MAYA
    (*small*) I'm scared.

MS. ASADA
    It's okay to be scared. It means something incredible is
    about to happen.

    MAYA goes.

OUTSIDE THE SUPERMARKET

*NAOMI collides with HIROSHI. They are both
dressed for winter. NAOMI has her personal
shopping cart.*

NAOMI
(*checking her phone*) Her phone just goes to voicemail.

HIROSHI
Naomi-san, you have to take care of our daughter. Promise
me you won't give up on her.

NAOMI
What are you talking about?

HIROSHI
I've always been a useless father. With both our children.
Worse than useless.

NAOMI
Stop.

HIROSHI
That Korean you don't like? The one who's been pestering
Maya online? I *hired* him to be friends with our daughter.

NAOMI
Why would you do that?

HIROSHI
You know that book I gave you?

NAOMI pulls the book out of her bag.

HIROSHI
(*finding the right page*) Here.

NAOMI
(*reading aloud*) "Perhaps the most powerful catalyst for change in *hikikomori* is romantic love, but for obvious ethical reasons it must never be induced within a clinical context."

HIROSHI
I was so stupid to think it could work.

NAOMI
No. Your plan *was* working, but I warned him away from Maya.

HIROSHI
You were trying to protect her. From me.

NAOMI
We just have to get in touch with that boy again. Where did you find him?

HIROSHI
"Better than real life." Ms. Asada. She knows where to find him.

NAOMI gives HIROSHI her personal shopping cart.

NAOMI

Here. Go wait at home for Maya. Take these groceries.

Without warning, HIROSHI hugs NAOMI, who shoves him away.

NAOMI

What are you doing? (*looking around, embarrassed*) What if someone sees us? They'll think we're two old people having an illicit affair.

HIROSHI

I love you!

NAOMI

(*straightening her clothing*) Yes. That's very nice. Call me right away if you hear from Maya.

NAOMI watches him leave.

GOODBYE

HIROSHI places his life-insurance papers in a large envelope on a table. He takes out his house keys and places them on top of it.

HIROSHI takes out his smartphone and records a message.

HIROSHI
Maya, I wish I could tell you this in person. I've never been ashamed of you. When we visited the Gundam statue in Akihabara, I'm not sure what I was expecting, but I have to admit I was a little disappointed. I mean, I didn't expect to see him transform into a spaceship and fly away. I guess I expected a little more movement than just his antenna splitting apart like that. Standing next to you, watching Gundam, I just wasn't impressed. But then when his breastplate lit up all neon pink, I thought, I know exactly how he feels.

HIROSHI stops recording.

HIROSHI turns off his phone, and carefully leaves it on the table next to his house keys and insurance papers. He walks out of his family's home, as if for the last time.

MS. ASADA

MS. ASADA is again concentrating on counting out a stack of crisp ten-thousand-yen notes before inserting them into colourful otoshidama New Year's envelopes.

An electronic bell chimes, and NAOMI enters.

NAOMI watches MS. ASADA for a moment, hesitant to interrupt.

NAOMI

Ms. Asada? Thank you for agreeing to see me on New Year's Eve.

MS. ASADA

Busy night for us. Lots of families getting together.

NAOMI

I won't take much of your time. I'm trying to find someone. I believe you met my husband, Tanaka Hiroshi?

MS. ASADA

(*looking up, surprised*) Oh, Mrs. Tanaka. Your daughter –

NAOMI

Exactly. I need to find Kilroy37. Can you tell me where he is?

MS. ASADA
(*writing on a piece of paper*) He's popular today.

NAOMI
(*reading the piece of paper*) "Dingo Manga Café."

MS. ASADA
You and your husband must be satisfied with the results?

NAOMI
Well, no. Things ended badly.

MS. ASADA
Oh Mrs. Tanaka, my condolences.

NAOMI
Sorry?

MS. ASADA
Your late husband.

NAOMI
Late? What are you talking about?

MS. ASADA
Forgive me. I misunderstood.

NAOMI
Misunderstood what?

MS. ASADA
Has your husband been acting differently lately? Is he giving away his belongings? Is he having mood swings?

NAOMI
Well, he ... (*touching her own arm*) Oh.

MS. ASADA
Mrs. Tanaka, do you know where your husband is?

NAOMI
He's at home.

NAOMI dials HIROSHI.

NAOMI
Voicemail. I need to go.

MS. ASADA
Of course. It's bad luck not to be with your loved ones at
the stroke of midnight.

NAOMI rushes out.

KONBINI

HIROSHI is in the konbini コンビニ *filling his plastic shopping basket with C.C. Lemon and a box of Pocky.*

DINGO MANGA CAFÉ

A hallway of doors. Pairs of shoes are neatly arranged outside each doorway.

MAYA pushes open the door to KENZO's cubicle. Laundry hangs. He is wearing boxer shorts.

MAYA's phone rings. She mutes it.

MAYA
Are you Kilroy37?

KENZO
Who wants to know?

MAYA
CobraKali.

KENZO
Kenzo.

MAYA
Maya.

KENZO
So this is me.

> *Gingerly, they move to touch each other, but it's too much. They act as if nothing has happened.*

MAYA carefully steps around KENZO's lair,
curious, but too disgusted to touch anything.

KENZO
Sorry, my maid is on vacation.

MAYA
Right, along with your mom's limo driver?

KENZO
Okay, so I'm not the first person to reinvent himself online.
The manager is on a smoke break, but I can give you the
rundown. The first hour is five hundred yen. They have
internet seat, love seat, reclining seat, massage chair, or flat
seat. All the PCs are equipped with Microsoft Office and
TV tuners.

MAYA produces the golden card and hands
it to him.

MAYA
Am I a job?

KENZO says nothing.

MAYA
Am I a job?!

KENZO
At first.

MAYA
At first?

KENZO

But then I started to like you. So I refused the payments.

MAYA

A great warrior doesn't require the best weapons.

KENZO

Said no one ever.

MAYA

You know what I hate most in this world?

KENZO

I didn't know how to bring it up. And then I thought, if I did, you would never talk to me again.

MAYA

That is the most intelligent thing you've ever said to me. Stay away from me.

MAYA's phone rings.

MAYA

(*into the phone*) Stop calling me!

NAOMI

Maya. Are you with your father?

MAYA

No, I left him with you. Where are you?

NAOMI

I am at home. Your father ... Maya. I am very worried.

MAYA
What? Why?

NAOMI
He left his keys. He left his phone. There's an envelope,
with a note that says, "Do not open until your first shrine
visit of the New Year."

MAYA
Open it!

NAOMI
It's his life insurance papers ... Maya. I think he's gone to
join your brother.

MAYA
(*to KENZO*) Put your pants on. You're going to help me.

KENO
Where are we going?

MAYA
Jukai.

JUKAI BOUND

MAYA and KENZO travel to Jukai.

NAOMI trails, not far behind.

Subway.

Three trains.

Bus ride.

Trailhead.

SCENE 29 (JANUARY 1)

FOREST

*In the darkness, HIROSHI comes to the edge of
the forest. He carries a backpack. He is exhausted
and dishevelled. He looks into the darkness
warily. He steels himself and disappears among
the trees.*

*MAYA and KENZO appear, using their
smartphones as flashlights.*

MAYA

How do you know he came this way?

KENZO

I don't. But this is the main trailhead everyone uses.

MAYA unfolds a paper map.

MAYA

I'll check out the Ice Cave. You look for him at the Wind
Cave. Here. He may be taking shelter there. After trudging
along a dark highway for three hours, that's what I would do.

KENZO

Trudging along a highway for three hours?

MAYA

He's retracing my brother's footsteps.

KENZO
    Got it. You okay?

MAYA
    If I can sprint the San Andreas Fault during a
    9.9-magnitude earthquake with flaming meteors raining
    down on my head and be god of the leaderboard for
    eleven days straight, I can hike through this forest.

KENZO
    We never played that game.

MAYA
    No, but I did.

        MAYA runs off.

THE HAUNTING

HIROSHI searches for the right place to die.
He is near the point of exhaustion. He hears
footsteps behind him, and he stops to look.
He sees nothing. When he resumes his search,
MAYA sprints up to HIROSHI.

MAYA
Dad!

HIROSHI
Maya.

MAYA collapses from exhaustion in his arms.

HIROSHI
You shouldn't have come.

MAYA
I know why you're here.

HIROSHI
You shouldn't be here.

MAYA
I was so scared. I've never been more scared in my life.
Scared of the darkness. Scared of the *yūrei*. Scared of
finding you too late. My heart was pounding so fast I
thought it was going to explode. And then I realized that's
what I wanted. So I ran harder and harder. I was chasing

(above) It's hard to learn from our parents, but even harder to learn from our kids. Maya wants her dad to see things differently.

(below) Do loved ones ever really leave us? Hiroshi holds up his son's favourite toy.

Photos: Raymond Shum

after my own death. That's when I remembered: It's okay to be scared. It means something incredible is about to happen. And then I wasn't scared anymore.

HIROSHI
You shouldn't have come. This is something I need to do alone.

MAYA
I felt his spirit, Dad. Running through the forest, I felt his spirit.

KENZO
(*off*) Maya!

HIROSHI
You hear that? Ichiro!

MAYA
No, Dad. That's Kenzo.

HIROSHI
Kenzo?

MAYA
The boy you hired. It's okay. I needed him to get here.

> *KENZO emerges from the forest. He watches them from a distance.*

> *MAYA reaches for HIROSHI's tattoo. A blast of wind rustles the treetops. MAYA looks up and around.*

MAYA

Ichiro is here. He brought you here. Can you feel him?

HIROSHI

What does he want us to do?

MAYA

(*closing her eyes for a moment*) He wants us to say goodbye. You can't let him go. I understand. But just know, whatever Ichiro is to you, your first-born, your only son, that is what you are to *me*. My only dad. And that's what I am to Mom. I'm her only daughter. If you leave us, just know that I will follow you, and then Mom will follow me. Ichiro is an anchor plunging to the bottom of the sea, and you have to let him go, because we're all connected. Let him go. Please.

NAOMI appears.

NAOMI

Anata! Buji de yokatta! あなた！ ぶじ で よかつた！

NAOMI embraces MAYA out of sheer relief, the first time they have ever hugged as adults.

HIROSHI

What are we going to do?

NAOMI

We can sell the house.

HIROSHI

Then how will Ichiro find his way home?

NAOMI
    Hiroshi. He's never coming home.

> *HIROSHI and NAOMI step away together, as*
> *HIROSHI finally unburdens himself of his*
> *backpack.*

> *MAYA steps away from her parents, and*
> *walks up to KENZO, who watches the horizon*
> *brighten.*

KENZO
    First sunrise of the year. Aren't we supposed to pray for
    something?

MAYA
    What could we possibly pray for?

KENZO
    I dunno. Good health, good luck, good family?

MAYA
    (*thinking for a moment*) I already have all that.

> *MAYA gives her map to KENZO for him to*
> *place it on her dad's knapsack, now perched*
> *on the ground. Out of his pocket, HIROSHI*
> *carefully places the Pocky on the knapsack.*

> *MAYA takes out her tattered photo of Ichiro,*
> *and places it on the knapsack.*

> *NAOMI reaches into her purse and produces*
> *Ichiro's favourite Gundam toy-robot model. Like*

a boy mesmerized by a new toy, HIROSHI takes it and begins to fly it skyward with the exquisite slowness of light speed toward the heavens. They all stare, as if watching a shooting star.

As a family, they all clap and bow toward the spirit of Ichiro. Together, they leave the forest.

END OF PLAY

AFTERWORD

INTERVIEW WITH THE AUTHOR
BY MARK ROBINS

A version of this interview was originally published by Vancouver Presents (*"Kuroko* Is a Journey from VR to the Scariest Place IRL,"* October 30, 2019).

Mark Robins: Tell us about *Kuroko*. What was the inspiration for telling this tale?

Tetsuro Shigematsu: When I was preparing for laser eye surgery several years ago, I knew I'd be out of commission for a couple of days, so I loaded up my phone with hours and hours of audiobooks. The experience of lying in complete darkness, with blackout curtains, not knowing if it was day or night, and spending all my conscious hours within imaginative worlds gave me a glimpse of what I suspect the future might feel like.

As we shift from the world of atoms and molecules to ones and zeros, our bodies have already begun to atrophy. We suffer from carpal tunnel syndrome, repetitive strain injuries, eye fatigue, text neck. Did you know that prison inmates, on average, spend more time outdoors than kids these days? But we voluntarily imprison ourselves, staring at screens like B.F. Skinner rats. I'm not a declinist. I don't think things were better in the past, but it does irk me when my kids would rather scroll through memes than go out for a bike ride with me.

Mark: Tell us about the significance of the title and how the *kuroko* feature in the play. Is it literal or metaphorical?

Tetsuro: *Kuroko* is a metaphor. Literally translated, *kuroko*

(黒子) means "black child," or "child of darkness," a rather poetic name for the stagehands in traditional Japanese theatre. The first time I watched a kabuki performance in Japan, I imagine my date must have found me rather annoying, with me nudging her every few minutes, asking, "What's the deal with all those ninjas on stage?" Clad entirely in black, audiences in Japan claim not to see them, as they occupy a culturally specific blind spot, in the same way that Western audiences pay no attention to the strings of marionette puppets. The shadowy *kuroko* enable players to achieve feats of virtuosity, and the otherwise impossible. So, to me, the *kuroko* is the perfect metaphor for this play. Who is the *kuroko*? Might there be a person in your life invisibly influencing your decisions?

Mark: Does it come from a personal interest in virtual reality?

Tetsuro: I think it's safe to say that for people below a certain age, say ninety, we are *all* interested in VR. But that fascination takes on very different forms. For example, my son has a keen interest in persuading me that five hundred dollars U.S. is not a lot to spend on the latest pair of state-of-the-art goggles. His is a very pragmatic interest in VR. As for me, my interest is more philosophical. Specifically, I'm interested in the promise of VR, which I think might just be the latest incarnation for that most ancient form of magic: the sense of wonder we feel when we wake up inside our dreams. Suddenly, we can fly, or indulge our most basic instincts without paying a price. Should people be allowed to act out their darkest fantasies? Could the virtual realm function as a pressure-release valve enabling us to act out antisocial impulses safely, or will it merely serve to amplify them like water on a grease fire? Pick your metaphor, because no one knows. So much of our daily behaviour is governed by duress. In the course of a day, we may want to stab this person or lick that person. We don't act on these impulses, because we know there will be a price to pay. But who do we become when there are no consequences? What happens when great sex becomes as easily accessible as a great meal? What will happen when people no longer require each other to satisfy their sexual urges? What if love and physical intimacy becomes a utility, like water, electricity, and our internet connection? To use Freudian terms, what happens when we become all id and no ego?

Mark: Aokigahara, or "Suicide Forest," plays a role in the play. What attracted you to this rather mythical place?

Tetsuro: Suicide Forest is notorious for being the most popular place to commit suicide in the world. It burst into wider public consciousness thanks to the infamous antics of YouTuber Logan Paul. What is less well known is that Suicide Forest, or, as it's known among the Japanese, Jukai 樹海, or "Sea of Trees," is that it is associated with the possibly apocryphal custom of *ubasute* 姥捨て. According to folklore, during times of famine, an elderly family member would be carried into the wilderness and left there to die. Japanese believe that Suicide Forest is filled with *yūrei* 幽霊, angry spirits, and is widely considered to be the most haunted place in all of Japan. Mythologically, as a place where many enter but fewer leave, Suicide Forest can be understood as an entrance to the Underworld, or Yomi 黄泉, the Japanese word for Hades.

For me personally, I'm curious about why this place at the base of Mount Fuji 富士山 has captured the imagination of a whole generation, why it has become part of the zeitgeist. Joyce Carol Oates wrote about boxing as an imaginative space where Americans tried to work out their ideas about race and class.* For me, Suicide Forest functions as an arena to think about suicide, death, and the real-world value we

---

* Joyce Carol Oates, *On Boxing* (New York: HarperCollins Publishers, 2006).

place on a human life. It's easy to make facile declarations about the infinite value of a single human life, but in practice that kind of idealism never manifests, certainly not in our justice system, not in our medical care. Every one of us assigns value based on gender, race, beauty, size, intelligence, attractiveness, wealth, and species. I've travelled to Suicide Forest. I've explored its paths and caves, and yet I still find myself lost in the labyrinth. Is suicide ever the right choice? Life is sacred, but what if delaying death increases suffering? Baby boomers – the generation that was never supposed to grow old – now face these very questions. Is it wrong for Japanese to sometimes consider suicide as a way of taking responsibility? Is our condemnation of such a calculus a form of ethnocentrism?

Mark: Your previous works, *Empire of the Son* and *1 Hour Photo*, featured you on stage, but this time you're allowing others to perform your work. What was it about this particular piece that made you decide not to also perform?

Tetsuro: I initially had hoped to perform in this play, but the playwrighting demands were such, it was decided I could be most useful if I focused myself entirely on the task of writing and rewriting. And rewriting.

Mark: Was that decision a difficult one to make?

Tetsuro: No, because it was made on my behalf. (*laughter*) Which is not to say it was imposed on me. Part of my way of working is to collaborate with people who are smarter than me. I want push back. I want productive tension. Because ultimately, we all want the same thing, for the work to be all that it can possibly be. What prevents a work from reaching its full potential isn't a lack of resources. It isn't a lack of money. Those factors are easy to blame. It shouldn't be a lack of imagination; otherwise what are we doing in this business? It often comes down to ego. I want it to be this way, because that's the way I originally intended, so don't mess with my baby. When our ego becomes an obstacle to change, that's when things go sideways.

Mark: You're in the rehearsal room with the actors and director. What's that process like as a playwright watching your work come together?

Tetsuro: It's fascinating to watch artistic specialists conjure meaning that was not intended, but is clearly encoded in the text. It makes you wonder about the subconscious creative process. I am of the school of thought that writers write to discover what they think about something. Under the guidance of a great director like Ami Gladstone, talented actors can amplify and illuminate those thoughts and ideas to levels where the playwright will be prompted to exclaim during the show, "That's genius!" But we're not talking about ourselves, we're referring to something more mysterious, a realm of creativity that lies *between* people and not innately. Given the autonomy of fictional characters, and the alchemy of actor and role, there is a hidden intelligence encrypted into scripts. A play can be much more clever than the person who wrote it.

Mark: What do you hope audiences walk away talking about after seeing the show?

Tetsuro: Have you ever decided to put your phone down for a minute and try having a conversation instead? Of course you have, but as simple as that sounds, that is a moment of awakening, a moment of clarity within our technologically induced slumber. It's like when you meditate, the moment you notice your mind drifting, that very instance is quite profound because you've become conscious of your consciousness, or lack thereof, even if it's just for a few fleeting seconds. I would love it if an audience member had just one moment like that, turning their phone off, and trying to be in the moment, the here and now with another human being. Which reminds me, I should probably go pump up my kids' tires. They're not going to be happy!

ACKNOWLEDGMENTS

To Jane and Ross

Whenever I have doubts about my calling, or my abilities as an artist, all I need to do is think of you two. "Surely, such beautiful, cultured, generous, and accomplished souls can't be wrong!" I love you.

To Yukari and Mark

If faithful support was a limited-edition print, yours would be marked in pencil thusly: "001" and "002." As a Canadian theatre artist, there is a limit to how far I can go in this world, but wherever I venture, know that it is your friendship that sustains me.

To Ken and Philip

During this pandemic, I've come to realize the only thing I truly miss are opening nights at the Cultch with you two, our favourite couple. Visions of finger food and sharing belly laughs in the lobby remain the light at the end of our tunnel.

To Mamiko and Makiko

I don't deserve the extravagance of your friendship, but it fills my heart with gratitude. Every *Nikkei* artist should have such stalwart allies, but when it comes to you two, I refuse to share!

To Nigel and Susanna

You two make me feel like I'm back in high school, but this time I'm in with the cool kids. Nicknames, texting, and Cardi B memes. I treasure your friendship.

My Olivia

Your words fall around me like flickering embers, comforting reminders that the bonfire of your everlasting friendship blazes throughout the night. Thank you for making me feel like I stand in the pantheon of the immortals.

To Donna

If I ever become successful enough to have envious enemies armed with a time machine, they won't have to go to the trouble of preventing my birth. They will just have to adjust the dial to Tuesday, June 21, 2011, at 3:10 p.m., and point out to you that I can't sing.

To Heather

All my life I've been a travelling minstrel. Because you so warmly welcome me to play in the courtyard of your castle, I feel like I have found my place in the world.

To Nicole

While my ilk struts and preens, you are the grown-up behind the scenes who makes all things possible. People like you are the true heroes of this world.

To Lisa

Consider this a platonic love note. We don't get to see you as often as we like, but know that when you're not around, we argue about who likes you more.

To Heidi

If anyone truly knows my work, they will think of you as often as they think of me. I thank my lucky stars that our orbits intersected, and that I get to continue on this artistic journey with you.

To Susan

When I'm an old man, some of my favourite memories will be walking home together with you after each show, the skylines ever changing, but you always the same, funny, insightful, and kind.

To Annie

When I heard it through the grapevine that you liked *Kuroko*, I was radiant. Such words coming from anyone else would have been insult-adjacent, but they were from you.

To Ami

Thank you for being the most generous collaborator. I am in

awe of not only your virtuosity as an artist, but your kindness as a human being. I bow full-*seiza* 正座 to you.

To Kevin, Vicki, and Spencer

One of the most unexpected pleasures of being a playwright is the gift of your family's friendship. Thank you for being so nice to me!

To Charles

Though our friendship has been almost entirely virtual, your charm, warmth, and intelligence shine through with every communication. Thank you for making this book so beautiful.

To the Chiefs

Kat, Trina, Jason, Jeff, Colleen

Of all the pins I wear upon my chest, the one that gleams most brightly is being able to call you my family. I left my heart in Treaty 6.

To Kalsang and Shaloh

Your friendship makes me a rich man. Brown bros for life!

To Jason

Thank you for redrawing the borders of faith in such a way that has allowed me to rethink my place in the cosmos. I'm proud to call you my friend.

To Ron

You're one of the finest men I know. Although we haven't spent much time together, know that your faithfulness, your humility, your artistry, your generosity, and your impulse to nurture fellow artists are traits I seek to emulate.

To George

If I had another son, you would be his namesake. Mercifully for him, that window is now closed, and "George Shigematsu" has been spared the burden of becoming someone so selfless, so kind, and so generous. What little masculine pride I have been able to salvage in my role as a provider has been due to your munificence. Thank you for taking care of my family.

To Taizo

Thank you for schooling me on gamer culture, the concepts, the terminology, the values, and the slang. If you are as patient with your children as you are with me, then my future grandchildren should have little to complain about.

To Mika

Your enthusiasm to make poster prototypes for "Suicide Forest" was the first inkling that this story might be intriguing. Your constant creativity inspires me. Thank you for being one of my favourite artists in the world.

To Yoshiko

When I look at Mika and Taizo, and the loving kindness they experience from their mom, I think, these are the luckiest children in the world. Then I realize, no, that title belongs to me.

Dear Bahareh

At the moment this was written, you were sitting next to Mika on the couch, ensuring she remained focused on her math instead of Instagram, freeing me to engage in the all-important work of penning skits to put on in barns. And then you walked in and showed me a photo from yesterday of Taizo pretending to stab me with your hunting knife as I lay suntanning on the shores of Alice Lake. Before long, my plays will gather dust on a "free-to-take" table, while our children venture through the world, grounded and content, thanks to the attentive heat of your love. Thank you for allowing someone as distracted and vainglorious as me to share this day-to-day existence with you, as you point out the more beautiful vistas of eternity.

TETSURO SHIGEMATSU was born in Beckenham, England. Christened as a baby in the Crown Court Church of Scotland, he began his career as a child preacher before finding his true path as a writer and performer. At the age of nineteen, he became the youngest playwright to compete in the history of the Quebec Drama Festival.

A former writer for *This Hour Has 22 Minutes*, Tetsuro's voice became familiar to Canadians when he took over hosting duties from Bill Richardson on *The Roundup* on CBC Radio, where he voiced nearly a thousand hours of network programming, as well as writing, producing and voicing over fifty pieces of radio drama. His editorial essays as a syndicated radio columnist which he wrote and performed won him two Radio Television News Directors Association industry awards for Best Commentary.

While based in Los Angeles, he made his debut as the impertinent samurai-in-residence on Spike/MTV's reality television hit *The Deadliest Warrior*, where he garnered an international following for talking smack and killing Vikings.

Dubbed "the voice of our Azn generation" by *Ricepaper Magazine*, Tetsuro's theatrical solo work *Empire of the Son* was named the best show of 2015 by the *Vancouver Sun* and has been touring continuously throughout Canada. It has played in eighteen cities to over twenty thousand people, and was described by Colin Thomas as, "one of the best shows ever to come out of Vancouver. Ever." The play also served as the centrepiece of his Ph.D. thesis at the University of British Columbia (UBC). His other solo work, *1 Hour Photo* garnered five Jessie Richardson Theatre Award nominations, winning for Significant Artistic Achievement, and was named as a finalist for the 2019 Governor General's Award for Drama. The *Georgia Straight* declared him "one of the city's best artists."

In 2018, Tetsuro earned his Ph.D. from UBC as a Vanier scholar. His unique ability to convey the complexities of race, ethnicity, and power in an accessible manner to vast audiences have made him the subject of numerous profile articles, and his growing body of work continues to be taught in university classrooms throughout North America as examples of possibility.